LOVE LETTERS FOR JOY

LOVE LETTERS FOR JOY

Melissa See

Library of Congress Cataloging-in-Publication Data available

ISBN 978-1-338-87538-6

10 9 8 7 6 5 4 3 2 1 23 24 25 26 27

Printed in Italy 183

First edition, June 2023

Book design by Cassy Price

To Tia Bearden:

For that morning in Tennessee,

when we were driving down the highway and you turned to me

and smirked.

We changed this book's entire plot in the span of

five surreal minutes,

just as our friendship changed my life.

I love you, sunshine.

A NOTE FROM THE AUTHOR

I've been disabled my entire life.

Many years into it, I realized that I also wasn't straight.

Disability and queerness are not mutually exclusive life experiences. You can be both.

You can take as long as you need to love those parts of yourself, too.

There are other disabled, queer people who will become your friends, and I promise, life will open up to you when that happens. We are a vibrant, eclectic community, and I love that I have been given the opportunity to embrace exactly who I am among them.

In writing this book, I wrote a love letter to my personhood. But I also wrote this story as a love letter to the disabled, queer people reading this. Because I am first and foremost a romance author—and disabled, queer people deserve happily ever afters.

And I want you to know: You are valid, wherever you are in your journey of navigating your intersectionality.

Now, before you dive into *Love Letters for Joy*, please be aware of the following content warnings: acemisia; anxiety; asthma attacks; brief mentions of religious bigotry; brief allusions to implied fertility issues; catfishing; discussions of divorce; familial emotional neglect; forced outing; homophobia; preterm labor and baby; queermisia; as well as a teenager being kicked out of their home. Please take care of yourself if you are not ready to read a book that contains this content. Joy, Caldwell Cupid, and I will be here when you are.

To: Valentina Ramirez (valentina.ramirez@caldwell.edu)
From: Caldwell Cupid (cupid@caldwellcupid.com)
Date: December 23, 7:15 a.m.
Subject: RE: Rockefeller Center Love Letter

Dear Valentina,
As requested, a copy of the love letter to your crush is attached. (Sorry it took me so long to get this back to you. I wrote many drafts until I felt it was right!)
Best of luck,
Caldwell Cupid 💘

Dear Yasmine,

You know me as a fun, bubbly extrovert, so in theory, it shouldn't be so hard for me to confess this. My feelings about you have blossomed—like the yellow tulips returning to Central Park in the spring—into something bright and beautiful, just like you.

I like spending time with you. I like walking home together. I like being near you. And of course, I like the friendship we've had for all these years. The single common theme through these experiences is just you, Yasmine.

I know Manhattan is a festive hellscape from now until New Year's Day, but I was wondering if you would like to brave the chaos together tomorrow, starting at Rockefeller Center.

Yours if you wish,
Valentina

CHAPTER ONE

JOY

My best friend Valentina Ramirez has been relentlessly tapping my shoulder for the past three minutes and forty-seven seconds. All because of this single sheet of paper that's figuratively burning a hole in her galaxy-print backpack.

Normally, I enjoy her enthusiasm . . . just when it's outside of school.

I adjust my circular tortoiseshell glasses and turn toward her, despite the fact that I can't afford to be distracted, especially not on the day before holiday break begins. We may still have six months left until we graduate, but the competition between me and Nathaniel Wright for valedictorian is tight—within tenths of a point. There's absolutely zero margin for error.

Nathaniel has been my undisputed academic rival for the last four years. We've also run the Caldwell Science Society together. He is the president, and I am vice president, and it's the only time we are remotely civil to each other.

"Joy." Valentina whines, leaning against her locker, her curly brown hair splaying out behind her. "I need to give Yasmine the letter. Today. Or my plans for an epic, touristy Christmastime date will be *ruined*. What should I do?"

Valentina has had a crush on Yasmine Crawford since Pride last summer, and she has finally worked up the courage to write to Caldwell Cupid, the anonymous student who spends all their free time writing love letters on behalf of the besotted at Caldwell Preparatory Academy. She received her letter before she was even out of her apartment this morning, so she has been a bundle of excited nerves ever since.

"Give her the letter when you see her in AP Biology?" I heft the straps of my rose-gold JanSport, wincing at how weighed down it is.

Valentina used to make fun of Caldwell Cupid with me. But lately she has been obsessed. It seems like the entirety of Caldwell Preparatory Academy is, actually. Everyone is so wrapped up in romance in a way that I understand from a scientific perspective but have little interest in otherwise.

Do I even want romance in my life? I'm on the side of the asexual spectrum that declares I do. But as I'm in the running to be the academy's first valedictorian with cerebral palsy, school comes first, so I've pushed it aside.

"I know that!" Valentina bursts, pulling me out of my thoughts and pushing her translucent blue cat's-eye glasses farther up the bridge of her nose. "But how?"

"We'll see Yasmine soon," our other best friend, Luca Sapienti, says, walking up to us. "I just saw her talking to Vikram about that cheerleading competition they have in January. Maybe use that as your opener?" He drapes his arm across my shoulders, pulling me into a hug. Luca and I have been friends since we were six years old, when my moms and I moved in across the hall from his family.

"Luca." Valentina blinks her luminous brown eyes at him. "Could you give Yasmine the letter for me?"

"Nope." He pops the *p* on the word. "I think you need to do this for yourself. It wouldn't mean the same coming from me."

"Joy?" She turns to me. "Could you?"

"I love you," I say, gently laying my left hand over hers. "But what logical sense would me giving a love letter to the girl you have a crush on make?" My fingers spasm, but since the three of us have been best friends for over a decade, it doesn't make me self-conscious.

"Joy!" Nathaniel's voice rings out through the hallway, practically making the spray of freckles across my nose go pink from embarrassment. "Good morning!"

Luca and Valentina smirk at me before stepping aside. My friends like to joke that Nathaniel and I are secretly in love with each other, and that our competition for valedictorian is "fueling the passion."

They couldn't be more incorrect, but I humor them anyway. It's easier if I just play along so that it's over faster and we can all get to class.

"Morning, Nathaniel," I reply as good-naturedly as I can muster.

Nathaniel strides over to me with long legs. Gorgeous enough to be a model, he has sky-blue eyes, a head of gold curls, and a jawline that could cut glass. He could have anyone he wants: an overly enthusiastic cheerleader, or the captain of the football team perhaps. But he's never actually dated anyone that I know of.

"Are you ready for our final meeting before break?" he asks loftily. "Mr. Baumann wants us to lead a discussion on cells, remember?"

"O-Of course I do." I look down at my gray pleated skirt, plum-colored blazer, white dress shirt, and the tie Momma fixes for me every morning. "I'm the one who suggested the topic."

Nathaniel's grin falters the slightest bit. "Only because you got a better grade than me on the paper about cellular structure." He's well over six feet tall, so as he bounces on the balls of his feet, his body tilts, shadowing my decidedly shorter frame. "You wanted to rub it in."

"It's okay," I mutter, my lips twitching. "You can admit that you're jealous of how I got a better grade than you."

"Joy." Nathaniel slowly stops moving his feet, placing his hand over his tie. "Are you suggesting it's my fault that autosave malfunctioned and deleted my notes on cellular structure in the first place?"

"No." My left hand twists into a knot, and I raise it up near my chest. "W-What I am suggesting, however, is that my understanding of cellular structure far surpasses yours and you just won't admit it."

Nathaniel's mouth drops open, and he staggers backward. "I didn't come here to be insulted," he grumbles.

"No, just to insult me because you can't stomach the thought that I'm better at something than you are," I retort.

"I only came over here to tell you I'm going to be late to club today," Nathaniel continues as if I hadn't said anything. "But only by a few minutes. I have a meeting with Miss Gupta to go over my academic progress." He raises one eyebrow. "Are you meeting with your guidance counselor, too?"

"I'm meeting with Mr. Moses the first week back." Each vertebra of my spine clicks into place as I straighten my back. "But my academic progress is excellent."

"Mine too," Nathaniel replies smoothly. "I'm only meeting with her to—"

"What difference does now versus January make?" Valentina asks, eager to have something besides her love letter to grasp on to. "It's the last day before break. C'mon, be realistic."

Nathaniel and I gasp, placing our hands over our hearts. "Every day of school matters," we say in unison as the bell rings.

"C'mon," I mumble, my cheeks warm. "Let's get to class."

When the four of us head upstairs to the science wing, Luca and Valentina look at me, their eyes gleaming in anticipation. Anticipation of *what*, though?

It's not like I'm going to run past Nathaniel and confess my love for him on the step above him like some weird academic homage to the balcony scene in *Romeo and Juliet*. Last year, Nathaniel and I had been chosen to read that scene in AP English and ended up arguing about line interpretation instead.

I mean, what does a pompous flirt genuinely know about romance, anyway?

"What?" My left hand contorts into a fist at my side.

"You know." Valentina smiles coyly when Nathaniel disappears up the next staircase after the landing. "Joy, maybe if you write a letter to Caldwell Cupid, then you can confess your feelings for Nathaniel."

"The ones you hold deep inside." Luca pats the Caldwell Preparatory Academy emblem on his blazer.

"You're ridiculous," I groan. "Both of you. But speaking of Caldwell Cupid." We reach the science wing, and it's my turn to smile at Valentina. "You need to give Yasmine your love letter."

Mr. Baumann's classroom is filled with silver desks, purple plastic chairs, and lab stations in the back. Colorful posters featuring diagrams of cells, the taxonomic ranks, and more pepper the walls. The biggest poster is an interactive one about DNA.

"Yasmine's not here yet," Valentina says, her excited nerves back again as we take our seats.

The door opens again, and I glance over Valentina's shoulder. A beautiful Black girl with a braided bun and lesbian pride flag earrings dangling from her lobes just walked in. "She's here now," I whisper. "Be assertive."

"Okay." Valentina blows out a breath from between her teeth, grabbing the neatly folded letter from her backpack's front pouch before getting to her feet. "Okay. I can do this."

"You can do this," Luca repeats bracingly. He turns to me; I see myself reflected in the lenses of his thick, square-framed black glasses. "Joy, show me your notes from yesterday so we can look distracted."

"Good idea." I unzip my backpack and remove my laptop. But instead of even turning it on, the two of us slowly scoot our chairs to the edge of the row so we can see.

"What happened to 'looking distracted'?" I whisper.

"We're three rows back from the door," Luca whispers back. "We'll be fine."

"Hi, Yasmine!" Valentina squeaks, both of them lingering by the doorway.

"Hey!" Yasmine smiles at her, ever the captain of the cheerleading squad. "What's up?" she asks when Valentina doesn't say anything next. "Did you need something?"

"Yeah." Valentina squeezes her eyes shut. "I—I needed to . . . Um." She awkwardly holds out the letter. "Give this to you."

"Okay," Yasmine says slowly, taking the paper and unfolding it. She scans the contents, her eyes growing wide. "Valentina," she murmurs, pressing the letter to her chest. "You really went to Caldwell Cupid to ask me out?"

Valentina studies her shoes, but nods. "Yes," she says. "Yes, I did. And—And you probably want a girlfriend who doesn't have someone else write a love letter, but I didn't know how else to ask you out. I'm not a words person; I'm a space person. The planetarium at the Museum of Natural History is my favorite place in the world, okay? You know that. Speaking of space, I forgot my astronomy textbook in my locker, and I have that next period because of course I took another science class as an elective, so, I'll just—"

Before she finishes her sentence, the bell dings again for the start of the day. But instead of coming back to her seat to sit with Luca and me, Valentina freezes, then bolts out of the room instead.

"Valentina!" Luca and I chorus.

"Val!" Yasmine calls, speed walking out the door after her. "Wait! Wait, hang on! Please!"

"Miss Ramirez and Miss Crawford!" Mr. Baumann sings, adjusting his glasses and rising from behind his desk. "Class has just begun!"

"One minute, Mr. Baumann!" Valentina's voice echoes faintly from down the hall. "Sorry!"

I turn to Luca. "That," I say, nodding toward the door. "Running away from a girl you just confessed your feelings to, while she chases after you. That's love?"

"I've never been in love." Luca shrugs, his skinny shoulders touching his pink ears.

"Me neither," I murmur.

"So how would either of us know?" Luca raises his eyebrows when Valentina and Yasmine walk back into the room.

Holding hands.

"We'll have to ask Valentina," I say, smiling at them as they sit down beside us.

CHAPTER TWO
JOY

At the end of the day, Luca, Valentina, Yasmine, and I head to the lecture hall in the science wing for our club meeting.

There are rows of silver chairs arranged in a circle facing a whiteboard. The modern lights hanging from the ceiling emit a warm glow, instead of the cold fluorescent lights used throughout the rest of the school. One wall is completely made of glass, looking out onto bustling Forty-Second Street below, while the other three are painted plum.

When the glass doors smoothly slide shut behind us, we're greeted by two voices.

"Hi!" Vikram Misra and Declan Turner wave from their seats at the very front. Declan is into cooking, Vikram is into theatre, but they joined our club anyway so that it could actually continue to exist. Declan also works at his family's Irish pub. Vikram is in every theatrical production Caldwell

Preparatory Academy puts on, and he is cheerleading co-captain with Yasmine.

The thought of juggling more than this club is enough to tangle my stomach up in knots.

"Welcome!" Mr. Baumann smiles from his spot, leaning against the whiteboard. He rolls up the sleeves of his white button-down, revealing a tattoo of the comedy and tragedy masks on his forearm. "We're just waiting for Nathaniel, then we can begin."

"How are the newest lovebirds of Caldwell Preparatory Academy doing?" Vikram beams at Yasmine and Valentina as we take our seats next to them.

"Another Caldwell Cupid success story, huh?" Declan ruffles his red hair, smiling.

"It's only been eight hours." Valentina smiles back, leaning her head on Yasmine's shoulder.

"We haven't even been on our first date yet." Yasmine balances their entwined hands on her knee as she grins as Valentina. "But just being *together* is pretty amazing, Val."

"Love that!" Vikram grins.

"Hey," Yasmine says, looking at me, Luca, and Valentina. "Do you mind if Nathaniel comes to the movie with us after school? We had plans, and I don't want to leave him high and dry."

"Sure, I think that's cool." Valentina glances at both me and Luca. Luca starts to nod, and I follow him, if only to distract myself from my stomach twisting at the thought of spending more time than is required with Nathaniel.

"It'd be entertaining to see Nathaniel and Joy go at each other outside of school, too." Luca chuckles, wincing as I elbow him in the side.

At that moment, the glass door opens again, and the sound of a certain pair of brown loafers sends irritated prickles down my arms.

"I have arrived!" Nathaniel says grandly. "Mr. Baumann, notice how I'm projecting my voice? I took your feedback from last week." When we discussed the taxonomic ranks, Nathaniel had to repeat himself twice in each category when explaining domain, kingdom, phylum, class, family, order, genus, and species. It was annoying when he mumbled, and it's worse now that he's shouting.

"I do, Nathaniel," Mr. Baumann tells him, nodding. "Very good job. Are you auditioning for *Pippin* after the break, then?"

"You should!" Vikram says excitedly. "Please! I've never been in a show with you before!"

Nathaniel pauses on his way to the front of the room, lingering right by my chair. "What's *Pippin*?" he asks innocently.

Mr. Baumann puts his face in his hands. "Remember the summer, Jonah," he whispers to himself. "You have community theatre during the summer.

"Anyway." Mr. Baumann claps his hands. "Now that

Nathaniel is here, we can begin the meeting. Everyone, today, we'll be learning about cells. Joy, Nathaniel, up front, please." Mr. Baumann steps aside as Nathaniel walks up to the whiteboard, and I join him.

"How would you like us to begin, Mr. Baumann?" I ask, turning to him.

"Hm." Our teacher taps his fingers on his chin. "I've got it." He grins broadly, his eyes gleaming. "You two are going to debate." He spreads his hands in front of him, as if encompassing the moment. "Scene: interior of a modest 1665 English countryside home. The two of you are a married couple who have just heard that cells have been discovered via a piece of cork."

"I'm his—" I barely choke out just as Nathaniel splutters, "She's my—"

"And!" Mr. Baumann continues. "You're of differing opinions as to whether cells are real or not."

"But of course, they—" both Nathaniel and I try.

"*We* know they're real." Mr. Baumann drops his hands, grinning. "However, seventeenth-century England was a different time, and there were plenty of skeptics back then, too. This will be a fantastic way to discuss scientific fact versus opinion!" He flops down in the nearest chair, his eyes bright as his red man bun bounces atop his head. "Action!"

Mr. Baumann really should be the theatre director instead.

I glance at Nathaniel, who seems frozen in place. He swallows hard, his Adam's apple bobbing.

"H-Husband!" I squeak, clapping my hand over my mouth on instinct. That single word reverberates around the room, flowing back into my ears, as if mocking me. Nathaniel's eyes go wide.

"Um." His voice is now so soft that I barely hear it even though I am only one step away from him. "Wife. You'll never believe what the townsfolk are discussing in the . . . the . . . uh . . . town square?" he continues. "Supposedly something called 'cells' have been discovered." He makes finger quotes around the word *cells*. "I choose to be a skeptic about this."

"A skeptic?" I lean against the whiteboard, folding my arms across my chest. "But why, um . . . Shouldn't we trust science?"

"You're a woman." Nathaniel makes a noise that's somewhere between a snort and a sigh. Either way, I've never heard him sound so disgusted. "What do you even know about science?"

"Oh crap," Declan whispers from behind us.

"Excuse me?" I push off the whiteboard to walk over to him, glaring up into his blue eyes. My left hand contorts into a fist, and I raise it to be level with my chest.

"Well, this is seventeenth-century England," Nathaniel replies. "Women of the time weren't literate, much less educated."

"Oh my God!" I shout, waving my palsied hand at him. "Tell me something."

Nathaniel's eyes glitter, a smirk curling his lips. "Gladly."

"Regardless of—of which century has the misfortune of putting up with someone at your level of *pompousness*—"

"You think I'm *pompous*?" Nathaniel looks off into the middle distance, as if this were the drama club instead and Mr. Baumann just gave him the direction to make this scene more engrossing. "Is that what we're calling *intelligent* now?"

"Nathaniel—" Mr. Baumann tries.

"He is smart," Declan whispers. "So is Joy, though."

"If you ask me, they're both a little much," Valentina adds.

"Especially together," Yasmine says.

"Are you actually this self-centered?" I step back, and Nathaniel's eyes return to mine. "Or does it only come out whenever *we* try to have a conversation?"

"Is this some sort of record?" Luca whispers. "Is this the fastest they've started arguing?"

"I think so," Yasmine whispers back.

"Oh!" Nathaniel laughs, his voice crackling. "So now I'm self-centered?"

"They're so dramatic, too," Vikram whispers. "They'd both be so good in drama club."

"They put on enough of a show," Declan says.

"Do you remember how you strolled into the room not

even five minutes ago?" I counter. "You're too pompous to see the world around you!"

"Holy shit," Luca whispers, barely hiding his laugh.

God, our friends' commentary is infuriating.

But I don't have time to focus on it because Nathaniel is even more so.

"Joy—" Mr. Baumann tries again.

"And you're too pompous to be comfortable with the idea of me being better than you at anything!" Nathaniel retorts. "It's like you can't even think that's a possibility!"

"Me?!" I yell back. "Which one of us couldn't handle the fact that I wrote a better paper on cellular structure?"

"Autosave malfunctioned!" Nathaniel shouts.

"Sure, a likely excuse. Who relies on autosave, anyway?" The fingers on my left hand dig into my palm, making me wince.

"All right, that's enough." Mr. Baumann appears between the two of us, and we bite back the rest of our words. "I encourage debate in this club. Not bickering."

"But—" Nathaniel splutters.

"Break it up and sit down," Mr. Baumann instructs.

"Mr. Baumann," I say once we're both seated on opposite ends of the room, directly across from each other, matched even when we're at odds . . . which is always. "You don't need to treat us like we're in first grade."

"Then stop acting like you are." Mr. Baumann leans against the whiteboard, rubbing his temples. "I've worked with my wife's elementary school students, and they're much better behaved than the two of you just were. Do you honestly think you're going to be able to run their science night in April? I'm going to need you to apologize to each other immediately." He gestures between us. "Whoever wants to go first."

A beat of silence passes. Luca slides his arm around my shoulders, and I lean into the comfort, taking a deep breath to steady myself.

"Joy." Nathaniel steeples his hands and balances his elbows on his knees. "I have a proposition."

"A proposition?" I repeat, moving Luca's arm off my shoulder as I straighten my back against the chair.

"Yes." Nathaniel nods, a smile back in place. "A bet, rather. I bet you can't beat me for valedictorian."

I stiffen, making the left side of my body spasm down my leg and up my arm. Luca notices and puts his hand on my arm. It calms me.

"Okay," I say. "And what will I get when I win?"

"Well." Nathaniel gets to his feet, walking purposefully toward me but stopping in the center of the room. "If I win, you have to give up your salutatorian speech. Instead, you'll just say"—he pauses to press his hand to his tie—"Nathaniel Wright, you are an academic genius, and it was an honor to try to keep up with you these last four years."

I raise my eyebrows. "When I win," I say, "you'll be the one saying those words. Except with my name."

Nathaniel smirks. "At the end of this year one of us will have to finally admit that the other is smarter. Does that seem fair?"

"Yes." I nod, feeling my own smirk flit across my face. "It does."

After Mr. Baumann dismisses the Caldwell Science Society, Valentina, Yasmine, Luca, Nathaniel, and I head to the Regal in Times Square.

"*Prism*?" Nathaniel looks at the framed poster of the latest Pixar movie as we're all getting drinks at the touchscreen soda fountains. The poster features a collage of rainbows and the protagonist, Delia, standing in the center of it, the lenses of her glasses splotched with purple.

"Yeah." Valentina takes a sip of her Grape Fanta and Coke. "We always see whatever Pixar movie is playing."

"This one's about a little girl who's an artist and explores her queer identity as she goes around New York City and encounters bursts of color," Luca adds.

Nathaniel pulls a face, but it's not out of disgust. It's contemplative, a look I see on him often enough not to be thrown by it.

"What is it?" Luca eats a handful of buttery, salty popcorn while we walk down the carpeted hallway of the movie theater, shrouded in its darkness and red walls. "Do you not like animated movies?"

"What?" Nathaniel blinks, shaking his head as we all sit in our recliner seats. I'll bet if he wore glasses, lights would be popping in front of his eyes. "No, it's not that. Joy?" He adjusts his seat, turning his eyes to me. "Do you want to come over to my house on Christmas to brainstorm ideas for the elementary science night?"

"Sure," I say. "S-Sounds good."

"Christmas?" Luca repeats. "So, you two won't even let yourselves enjoy the holiday?"

"Leave them alone." Yasmine nudges him. "If they want to do schoolwork on Christmas, they can."

Just then, my phone vibrates with a text message. I flip it to silent but tap the notification.

Valentina (4:55 p.m.): Yasmine, should we change our plans to a double date tomorrow?

Yasmine (4:55 p.m.): I mean, we artfully arranged for Joy and Nathaniel to sit together. So probably.

Joy (4:56 p.m.): Absolutely not. You don't need me tagging along to ruin your date.

Luca (4:56 p.m.): All they'd do is argue about the science of animation or something.

Luca (4:57 p.m.): Stop teasing Joy. You're making her uncomfortable.

Joy (4:58 p.m.): Thanks, Luca.

I dig into my Cookie Dough Bites, grateful for the help that chocolate and sugar provide.

A preview plays for some rom-com where an overworked woman in her thirties will most certainly fall in love with her best friend by the end—and Luca's hand brushes my left.

"Joy," he whispers. "You don't ruin things."

I squeeze his hand—whether out of relief or involuntary muscle contractions, I'm not sure—eating another handful of candy.

"Thank you," I whisper back, "for being such a good friend."

"I just want you to be happy." Luca pulls his hand back behind his armrest. "Yasmine and Valentina want that, too."

"I know," I whisper. But suddenly my chest goes a little tight, and I think about the acceptance letter from the California Institute of Biology sitting in my inbox.

In less than a year, I'll be living clear across the country from my friends—and I haven't told them yet.

Will they still want me to be happy when I do?

CHAPTER THREE

CALDWELL CUPID

To: Caldwell Cupid (cupid@caldwellcupid.com)
From: Anonymous (anonymouscaldwell@mailthis.com)
Date: December 23, 7:49 p.m.
Subject: I Like Someone

Dear Cupid,

I can't believe I am sending this email, but since I might be running out of time, here goes. I like someone. She goes to school here, and we've known each other for a long time.

I was never much of a fan of this anonymous account, but I need your help. Please write me a love letter for her.

Thank you,

Anonymous

I stare at my computer, rereading the email that I've just received. But, as I'm trying to figure out how I can even begin to write the love letter this person is requesting, I stare so long that the screen goes fuzzy in front of my glasses.

It's not that this student kept their name anonymous; sometimes people do that, keep their names to themselves.

It's the fact that they didn't give me any specific details.

I can't exactly craft romance without specific details.

Groaning, I rub my eyes, pushing up my frames. When I lean back in my leather desk chair—one that boasts lumbar support but is doing absolutely nothing—Declan Turner lobs a piece of crumpled-up notebook paper at my head.

I whirl around, the motion nearly knocking my rescue inhaler off my desk. "What was that for?"

Declan smirks. "I need advice. And I couldn't get your attention."

"Advice?" I repeat, as if I don't dole out advice every single day. "On what?"

Declan raises his red eyebrows, pulling a face. "It's about . . . I like someone?"

Oh, for Christ's sake. How am I supposed to skirt around this?

"Ah, yes."

With dramatics, apparently.

I press my hand to my heart, looking longingly into the middle distance. The deep red cashmere sweater, which is so much nicer than the school uniforms, is soft under my fingers.

"As I am the only person you've ever dated," I continue loftily, "I suppose I'm the only place to go for this kind of advice."

"Listen to you." Declan chuckles. "Do you *miss* me already?"

"I'm flattered." I laugh. "Truly, I am. But I broke up with you, remember?"

"Of course I do." Declan shrugs. "We're better off as friends anyway."

For months, Declan and I hooked up wherever we could: empty classrooms, secluded staircases, our bedrooms on the weekends.

But it was a secret.

Declan's already out to his parents. He baked them a rainbow Funfetti cake with the words HI, I'M GAY written in blue frosting across the top. But I haven't had that conversation with my family. The only one who knows I'm pansexual is my sister, and she lives in Murfreesboro with her husband.

I didn't want to feel like I was forcing Declan back in the closet with me, so I ended things. Everyone has different views on coming out versus staying closeted, but I knew what I wanted for myself.

"Besides," Declan continues as I join him on my navy-blue bedspread, "I like someone else now."

"Who?" I ask, drawing my long, spindly legs up to my chest.

Declan smiles to himself, as if I'm not even here. "Eitan Simon," he replies. "He's in my AP English class."

"Oh, he is cute. He has a good voice for Shakespeare, too," I say. "Are you going to ask him out?" I grin back at him. "What's the plan?"

Declan thinks for a moment, tapping his freckled chin. "I might write to Caldwell Cupid and ask for a love letter."

It takes all I have not to laugh. Declan has no idea I'm Caldwell Cupid.

"If you want to," I find myself saying. "They answer everyone back, right?"

"We're home!" I almost fall off my bed at the sound of my mother's voice. I didn't realize my parents would be back from work so early; they were scheduled for an overnight shift at the hospital. "Please come downstairs!"

"Sounds urgent." Declan gets to his feet, cracking his back. "I'll see myself out."

We say goodbye in the entryway, and I head into the living room. My family turns to look at me, their gazes dappled by the city lights streaming through the windows.

I jolt, realizing everyone is here. Mother and Father are still in their blue scrubs. My brothers, Warren and Everett, are wearing jeans and gray sweaters, making me wonder if they color coordinated before coming over.

"What's going on?" I ask. "Are Francine and Richard okay?"

"Richard." Warren scoffs from his place in the oatmeal-colored armchair. He's the broadest of us, nearly filling up the seat with muscles alone. "If he ever comes here, I'm—"

"Warren." Father raises a hand to silence him before turning to me. He never lets his anger boil over. You can only tell his emotions by the way his mustache moves. And it's twitching.

"They're divorced!" Mother wails. She, on the other hand, is very comfortable letting her feelings boil over.

My mouth falls open. "They're what?!" I look at each of my family members in turn. "I thought they were coming for Christmas?"

"If he had the nerve to show his face here, we'd leave him at LaGuardia," Everett chimes in. "No, he's staying in Tennessee—"

"They've been divorced for months!" Mother continues as if Everett hadn't even spoken. She takes her phone out from the pocket of her scrubs. "Francine just told us."

Father sighs. "Be that as it may," he says. "Francine will be moving back in with us until she finds a place and a new job. She's an accomplished pediatrician. I'm sure it won't be long until she's settled."

"Back home." Mother sniffs, leaning against Father and turning her face into his shoulder. "With us."

"Was that . . . everything?" Warren asks, sighing. "Belinda wants me to wrap extra presents. I need to get home."

"Go, go," Father says, barely looking at him. All his attention is on Mother. "We'll see you later."

I'm still in a little bit of a daze as I head back upstairs to write my next Cupid email. Why would anyone want to fall in love and get married when it can end in a flash?

I sit at my desk, put on my blue light glasses, and open the email. Still vague, still nothing to go off of. But I have a reputation to uphold, so I start to compose a reply.

To: Anonymous (anonymouscaldwell@mailthis.com)

From: Caldwell Cupid (cupid@caldwellcupid.com)

Date: December 23, 8:30 p.m.

Subject: RE: I Like Someone

Dear Anonymous,

I can't very well write a love letter to someone if I don't know anything about them. So, tell me, what is her name? And what are some of your favorite things about her? Why do you like her?

Best of luck,

Caldwell Cupid

CHAPTER FOUR

JOY

Christmas Eve is the biggest day of the year for my family.

Ma putters around our postage-stamp-sized kitchen with her Christmas playlist cued up as she cooks everything from chicken Parm to a chocolate-raspberry cake shaped like a Christmas tree. Momma, on the other hand, is there as her third and fourth arms until it's time for her to make the ribs. Ma is from an Italian American family whose lineage she's traced back to when her ancestors immigrated. Momma is from a family in Tennessee with their own chain of barbecue restaurants—and she wins the FDNY cook-off every year because of it. So naturally, they're very good at making enough food to feed the entirety of our Manhattan apartment building. It's just what they do.

But me? I'm in my room studying until it's time for the party.

"Joy Elise!" Momma calls in her honeyed Southern voice,

knocking on my bedroom door, practically scaring me out of my gold Mary Janes. My copy of *Advanced Biology* almost falls into my lap, but I grab it with both hands.

"Yeah?" I reply, hefting the huge textbook back on my desk and smoothing out the skirt of my wine-colored dress.

Momma opens the door, the sounds of Bing Crosby's "White Christmas" flooding my ears. Pomegranate, our three-legged black cat, propels herself into my room, jumping up onto my meticulously made bed with its lilac pillows and matching comforter in precisely the correct places. Well, they were before she hurled herself onto them.

"Are you ready, baby?"

"Is it time already?" I spin my desk chair toward my window. Union Square is dark, as dark as the city gets in the winter with its ever-present twinkling lights.

When did that happen? I guess I didn't notice because—

"No!" I spring to my feet with enough force to smash my knees on the underside of my desk, nearly keeling over from the sharp pain I've inflicted upon myself.

"Are you okay?" Momma asks, gently grabbing my arm to steady me. "What do you mean, no? You look beautiful."

"It's not that." I look over at her. We are almost mirror images. We share the same short red hair and smattering of freckles. The only difference between us is the color of our eyes. Hers are hazel, mine are blue, courtesy of my sperm donor father, whoever he is.

"I mean, thank you. But no. I—I forgot to get Luca a present. I already got Valentina's and Yasmine's." For Valentina, a pair of Mercury bookends, her favorite planet. And for Yasmine, a cute pair of strawberry earrings. "I meant to go get something for Luca before the party, but I got so wrapped up in schoolwork. Is their door open yet?"

Every year for Christmas Eve we have a floor party where our families leave their doors open and people drift between our units. It's been tradition ever since my moms got married and moved into the building. Luca and I exchange gifts at this party every single year.

"Oh." Momma's face falls as she runs a hand through her hair. "Well, I'm sure you could go shopping tomorrow morning."

"No." I scratch at the buzzed sides of my pixie cut. "No, no. It has to be now. Look, Barnes and Noble is just down the block. I'll be real quick. Promise."

"All right." Momma sighs, her laugh lines crinkling. "Just take your coat. Ma wouldn't let me hear the end of it if you went outside without it."

"Thank you!" I fling my arms around her, and she cocoons me in her warmth for a brief second. "Ma, I'm going shopping!" I yell as I run down the hallway, my feet slipping around in my shoes. "I'll be back!"

Ma pokes her head out from the serving hatch, her dark brown bun hanging at the nape of her neck. "Coat, hat, *and* gloves!" she says, waving her oven mitt at me as I dive into the closet. "We love you."

The yarn from my ace pride scarf gets stuck in my mouth as I wrap it around my face. "Love you, too."

If I thought Christmas Eve was hectic in my apartment, it's nothing compared to the Barnes & Noble in Union Square. It's a huge store that towers over my neighborhood with four floors of books and shelves that stretch up to the ceiling. And—something my exhausted cerebral palsy legs are thankful for the existence of every time I see them—escalators to every level.

I'm sagging against the escalator railing as I head up to the top floor where the manga and graphic novels are. Luca's a dork in every sense of the word, including his expansive manga collection. But I've seen his shelves enough times in my life to have all the volumes he owns memorized, so I make mental notes of his inventory as I stroll through the stacks.

The first volume of *The Poison King* is displayed face out, showcasing a deep purple cover and a handsome king with bright purple eyes. Luca doesn't have this yet.

I'm reaching for it when I hear an all-too-familiar voice from the next aisle over that makes my fingers slip.

"I know. I won't be long."

Ugh, what's Nathaniel doing here? Last-minute shopping? Typical of someone so self-centered.

I'm rooted to the carpet because of a muscle spasm that has

chosen this exact moment to snake down my left side, but also because I have no idea what I'll say to Nathaniel if he sees me.

"I'm aware that it's the holiday season, I will be sure to pick out just the right thing," Nathaniel continues. "I'll be back soon."

I know he's about to turn and see me, but I still can't bring myself to move a muscle.

"Joy?" Nathaniel yelps my name when he rounds the shelves, and our eyes meet.

"Hi, Nathaniel." I grab the first volume of *The Poison King* just so I have something to do with my hands. His eyes flick down to the cover, then back up to me, his pupils widening for a second. I doubt he's ever seen me with a book other than a textbook or assigned reading from English. "It's Christmas Eve. What are you doing here?"

"I could ask you the same question." Nathaniel's shoulders are stiff beneath his khaki peacoat, pushing out the simple brown scarf tied around his throat. He fixes his smirk back in place. "What are *you* doing here?"

I step forward, the volume of manga bending against my chest. "I asked you first."

"That's true," Nathaniel says thoughtfully. The tip of his tongue pokes out the side of his mouth, sweeping across his bottom lip. "Well, I'm here to buy a present." He holds out an enormous black leather-bound book with gilded silver edges. *Gray's Anatomy* is printed across the front with a silver stamp of lungs just below it. "For myself," he adds.

"A text on human anatomy from the nineteenth century?" I trace the design of the lungs with my eyes, then look up at him.

I have the same book in my bedroom, which throws me.

"Well, it's our senior year," he says. "I'm looking into all my options. I can do anything, go anywhere. Dr. Wright... Doesn't that have a nice ring?"

Nathaniel's confidence pricks at my skin. He isn't afraid of following any dream, even if that takes him away from the friends he knows.

Nathaniel blinks at me, completely silent, so that I can experience my existential crisis in peace. Or maybe just so that I can explain what I'm doing in a bookstore on Christmas Eve.

"That's... really nice." My tongue sticks to the roof of my mouth with each word. "Do you. Um. Know what specialty you might want to go into?"

"Not yet." Nathaniel's eyes drift down to his shiny brown loafers. "But I have four years of premed biology before I need to decide." He glances up at me, a flicker of light in his gaze. "Do you know what you're going to study after we graduate?"

"Oh." I nod, my left hand curling in on itself. "Yes. I-I'm going into nursing, to be a NICU nurse, like my ma."

Nathaniel goes quiet. Too quiet. He's probably taking his time to silently judge me. I bet he is thinking, *A nurse. Not a doctor.*

"Well," he says finally, "I think that's perfect."

I stare at him. "What makes you say that?"

"Because, Joy." Nathaniel smiles, just a glimpse of white teeth through pink lips. "Then, even after graduation, we'll be on similar paths. Which means our competition can continue."

"You can't throw me off," I tell him. "That valedictorian spot is mine."

"We'll see about that," Nathaniel says, extending his hand to me. "I hope you're practicing your lines for when you lose."

I take his hand in mine, marveling for the briefest of moments at how warm it is despite the freezing temperature outside. "I didn't even bother committing them to memory."

We shake once and drops our hands.

"Anyway." Nathaniel clears his throat. "Um. Are you buying a present for yourself as well?"

"No." I hold out the volume of *The Poison King*, watching as his eyes rove over the cover, taking in every detail of the gorgeous artwork the same way I took in the lungs on the cover of *Gray's Anatomy*. "It's for Luca."

Nathaniel's eyes snap to mine. "Luca?" He repeats the name as if it's a person he doesn't know.

"Yeah." I tuck the book against my chest. My ace pride scarf itches my neck, and I tug at it with my left hand. "Our families celebrate together, and we exchange gifts."

"Oh."

When I look up at him, his eyes aren't on mine. They're studying my spastic left fingers tangled in the yarn of my scarf. As though he doesn't see me spasm every day.

"Well, that's nice," Nathaniel says, glancing down at his phone, which has started to vibrate. "I need to get going. I might throw this thing into the Hudson if I get one more text." He chuckles. "Hang on. Hey, you should give me your number, and I'll text you my address for tomorrow."

Before yesterday, I would've thought having his number in my phone would be the definition of absurd. But now I try to tell myself that punching in Nathaniel's name and number is logical and not ridiculous.

We slip our phones into our coat pockets and stand awkwardly for a moment. I'm not sure how to end this interaction. Nathaniel steps forward. Just as I think he's about to walk past me, he leans down and kisses my cheek. "Merry Christmas."

For a moment I am shocked silent. His lips were soft, if a little chapped from the winter air. "Merry Christmas," I reply faintly, spinning on my right heel and heading toward the escalator, thoughts swirling through my mind.

CHAPTER FIVE

CALDWELL CUPID

Mother's heels clack as she paces back and forth across the living room, wringing her hands. The party is supposed to start any minute, but we're still waiting for Francine to arrive from the airport before we leave.

"I cannot believe this!" Mother stops in front of the Christmas tree, backlit by its collection of multicolored lights. She might start eating the popcorn and cranberry garland string around it—that's how nervous she is. "Why didn't she let us come get her? Why does she insist on using Lyft?"

"Maybe because it's Christmas Eve, and this city is already hectic enough?" I offer from my seat on the couch. I want to loosen my tie, but I don't move my hand because if I show even the slightest sign of being worried about my sister, then Mother will be even more upset.

"He's right," Warren says, his arm around his wife, Belinda.

"Don't worry, Grandma!" their son, Caleb, encourages. He and his twin sister, Cara, are in the middle of playing their third, heated consecutive game of Candy Land. (I have never been so thoroughly defeated in a board game as I was moments ago when I joined in for their second one.) "I-I'm sure Auntie Franny will be here soon!"

"Thank you, love!" Mother tries to smile, but the edge of her mouth twitches until her lips are pursed closed. "You are probably right."

"I also think Auntie Franny will be here soon!" Cara adds, pitching her voice high. "That means it has to be true, Grandma!"

"Does it now?" Mother says, her tension easing as Father pulls her to his chest. Tonight, they're wearing a blouse and button-down in matching shades of red. I guess the color was an accidental theme.

"Anna," Father murmurs. "Francine is an adult. She's perfectly capable of getting things done herself." He kisses the top of her head. "You know that. I know you do."

Mother sighs. "I know, Victor. It's more . . . the *divorce*." She says it like it's a curse word she doesn't want Cara or Caleb to repeat.

"Mother," Everett huffs from the armchair. "Would you prefer she stayed with that asshole?"

"Everett!" Mother hisses. "Language!"

"Curse words count as language," I reply, earning a smirk from both of my brothers and sister-in-law.

Mother clucks her tongue, moving away from Father, but not so far away that they let go of each other. "I suppose so," she replies. "And of course, Francine shouldn't have *stayed* with him. My daughter knows her worth."

"She does," Father agrees.

"I'm just so worried about how this is going to affect her," Mother continues. "I mean, she loved Richard so much that she moved away from New York to be with him."

"Plenty of people move away from home when they grow up, Mother," Everett points out. "At least Franny isn't across the ocean, like Douglas Moray-Porter's brother. He moved to Scotland."

"Yes, but at least he's still married. Those poor parents." Mother sighs. "First, Douglas comes out, and then Gavin moves across the ocean."

My insides tighten and push my heart up into my throat, where it sits like a stone. Those kinds of offhand comments are why I haven't come out myself.

"Both Douglas and Gavin are happy," Everett says. "Isn't that what matters most? There is nothing wrong with moving away or with being gay." His words help my heart find its way back into the safety of my rib cage.

"Of course," Mother murmurs. "I just . . . A mother worries about her son's friends. That's all."

"A father, too," ours adds.

"Douglas and Levi are happily married, so I think they're doing just fine," Everett says.

"Oh." Mother purses her lips like she just swallowed a lemon, seeds and all. "Well, that's wonderful."

Thankfully, there's a knock at the front door, and Mother flits away to answer it.

"Francine!" she coos. "Honey, come inside!" She flings the door open, and where there should be more noises—of hugs, of chatting, of Mother fawning over her—there's just silence.

Those of us left in the living room glance at one another, then move into the hallway as if we were a single organism.

"Mother, can I come in?" Francine asks her gently. "Please."

As if her bones had been replaced with wood, Mother moves stiffly aside.

Francine's blond hair is pinned up and away from her face, and she's wearing a puffy black jacket with a gray faux fur hood, unzipped and revealing a pregnant belly.

"Explain." Mother's voice sounds like it got lost on the way out of her mouth.

"You're pregnant," Father says.

"About five months along now," Francine replies, taking off her coat and folding it over her arm. Her green maternity sweater clings to her stomach.

"We're just finding out about this now?" Father asks. "You

do realize that you're going to give birth in approximately four months, correct?"

"And you *flew* here," Mother adds. "Do you realize how foolish—"

"She's fine to fly until she's thirty-six weeks along," Warren cuts in. "You're both focusing on the wrong thing. She's here safe, isn't she?"

"I am." Francine sighs, accepting Everett's offer to hang up her coat. "I need to sit down."

"Here." Everett clears a seat on the couch for her and gets the ottoman situated under her feet.

"You don't need to explain anything, Franny," I say, finally finding my voice as I sit down on the couch.

"Thank you." My sister gives me a soft look, one that makes her eyes glassy with tears she wipes away. "But no," she murmurs. "I should."

"Only if you want to," Belinda says gently. She and Francine are best friends, the reason she and Warren were even introduced in the first place.

"I do," she begins. "Well, for starters, after I learned I was pregnant, we separated. I finalized the divorce as quickly as I could, and now I'm here."

"But why didn't you tell us?" Mother asks. "We haven't had time to prepare anything."

"When I tell people I'm pregnant is my decision." Francine places a hand on her stomach. "It's not for other people's comfort. But you're right that nothing is prepared, I'll give you that."

"We'll help you however you need," Warren says, glancing around the living room.

"We are not at all prepared for this," Mother squeaks, her voice getting higher. "Everett, sweetheart, you're the next to get married, so when you do, please don't *abandon* your wife—"

"Mother!" Warren, Everett, and I all snap at the same time. She turns back into Father's shoulder and starts to cry.

"She's correct," Father says. "None of us were expecting Francine to be pregnant."

"*I'm* prepared for this," Franny points out, her voice shaking just slightly. "And I think that's the paramount thing to focus on here." She exhales, gazing down at her belly as she pats it. "Any more stress than I'm already under could be bad for both me and my daughter, so please let's all just . . ."

"Change the subject?" Everett suggests, sitting next to Franny and putting his arm around her.

"Yes." Franny nods. "That sounds like a great idea. So, how's your new position?"

"Oh." Everett smiles, dimples deepening in his pink cheeks. He recently transferred from his hospital in Washington Heights and is now a pediatric surgeon in Union Square. "It's been wonderful. I'll see if there are any openings for a pediatrician if you'd like."

"That would be great!" Franny grins back at him. "It

would be so nice to work in the same hospital after years of being away."

"About that." Mother sighs, her voice weary and wet. "Everett, I don't see why you had to transfer hospitals. St. Thomas's is very well respected."

"You have to say that because you're friends with people on the board of directors," Everett replies, his smile drying up instantly. "I'm in my thirties and I get to choose where I work."

Mother and Father both open their mouths to speak, but Warren gets to his feet before they can formulate words. "Let's actually get going to the Christmas party," he says. "Shall we?"

CHAPTER SIX

JOY

I'm breathless from rushing back home to wrap Luca's gift. The moment I step through his door, Luca offers me a mug shaped like a snowman. It's filled to the brim with his mom's Crock-Pot hot chocolate. The thick, warm scent of milk and dark chocolate, with hints of vanilla and salted caramel, fills my nose. It's almost enough to chase away the cold from outside.

"Thank you." I smile a little as my muscles relax.

"You're welcome." He grins. "Our parents are in your unit, busy with chicken Parm and apple cider hot toddies. You wouldn't believe the chaos around here earlier." He gestures to the glittery snowflake-patterned bag in my hand. "Is that for me?"

"Yes." I sigh.

Luca's smile is as bright as the Christmas tree in his living room. "Thank you." He bounces on the balls of his feet, purposely jingling the bells of his ugly Christmas sweater. He buys a new one every holiday. This year, it's a monstrosity of Santa's sleigh and his reindeer, where each piece is made of felt and accompanied by a bulbous gold bell. "Can I open it now?"

I take a sip of hot chocolate, closing my eyes at its richness. "Since you brought me hot chocolate," I say, "yes."

"Yay," he says. "Let's go to my room just in case our families decide to come back."

After ducking into the living room to grab my present, Luca leads us through the kitchen and down the hall to his bedroom. His bed is unmade, with its red comforter shoved toward the bottom. His room is lined with anime wall scrolls, and there's a small bi pride flag pinned above his headboard.

He sits in his padded red gaming chair, spinning it away from his three computer monitors, instead facing me and his bookcase stocked with manga.

"Here." I hand him his present. "Merry Christmas."

"Yes!" He grins at me as he takes the volume of manga from the bag. "I've wanted to read this, thank you! Open yours now."

Sitting on his bed, I carefully start to unwrap mine, my throat going tight as I touch the soft purple fleece of an NYU sweatshirt.

"Luca." His name is soft in my suddenly dry mouth.

"Do you love it? When I got my NYU Courant acceptance, I went out and got one for myself immediately." He places his hand on my knee. "So when you get accepted to NYU nursing, we can match!" A blush paints Luca's cheeks—it's even across his nose. "I got Valentina a Barnard one, and I was wondering if you wanted to split an NYIT one for Yasmine. I think it would be nice if we got her something, you know?" He falls quiet, gazing at a picture of me, him, and Valentina on his nightstand. It's a group selfie taken at Pride last summer, all three of us with our respective colors painted on our cheeks and flags draped across our shoulders.

At that moment, our phones chime with texts from our group chat.

Yasmine (7:07 p.m.): Merry Christmas Eve! 💖🎄

Valentina (7:07 p.m.): Check our Instas! 😌

"I'm glad they're finally together," he says.

"They've been crushing on each other for months now," I add.

"Longer, actually." Luca stretches his free arm above his head. He plops down on his bed beside me as we each open

Instagram. "Which you'd know if you actually took a break from studying."

"Don't change the subject." I playfully smack his arm and he smirks.

"Seriously, though." Luca rolls his eyes, his voice going quiet. "You spend all your time on this competition with Nathaniel."

"Luca," I sigh. "I have to win. You know how important valedictorian is to me!"

"I know." Luca tries to chuckle. "I'll hack into the school system to make you valedictorian if I have to."

"Don't be ridiculous." I nudge Luca's phone with mine, showing him a selfie of Yasmine and Valentina beaming in front of the Christmas tree at Rockefeller Center. They're both wearing puffy coats, paired with matching green-and-red-striped scarves peeking out from their coats. Valentina is kissing Yasmine on the cheek, while Yasmine has her arms wrapped around her.

Suddenly I'm thinking about Nathaniel's lips on my cheek less than an hour ago.

But I'm not telling any of my friends that happened. They would never let me live that down. Nathaniel and me having the tiniest amount of physical contact would be nothing short of hilarious and make Luca laugh enough to need his inhaler.

I shake my head, reading Valentina's caption:

Valenspace

374 likes

Spent Christmas Eve morning with my girlfriend! It took me long enough to ask her out, but I'm so excited that we're together now! Missing you already, @yasminelynn. 😮 Can our next date be somewhere warm, please? Thank you, #caldwellcupid!

"Are you okay, Joy?" Luca's voice jolts me back to his bedroom.

"Yeah." I clear my throat against the sleeve of my dress, staring at the raised arm hair beneath the lace, even though I have no reason to be cold. "Why?"

"Just seemed like you weren't here." Luca shrugs, moving his thumb across his phone screen. "Look. There are more photos."

Even though I could just look at my own phone, I lean over to watch as Luca scrolls through the pictures. Valentina and Yasmine ice skating. Valentina and Yasmine sipping hot chocolate. Valentina and Yasmine kissing in front of the Macy's windows—which this year are decorated in the theme of Mickey and Minnie Mouse.

Their happiness glows brighter than the lights and holiday cheer around them. I've seen this look on Luca's face before, too, when he'd dated Hanna last year. His promposal had involved filling both the hallway and their shared locker with roses, which we'd all helped with. If she hadn't moved to

Orlando for college, they would probably still be together and have their own bevy of selfies for Instagram.

I look up from his phone. It hits me then: I've never had that look on my face before. I've been so focused on school that I never even gave myself the option. An odd sensation blooms in my chest, one that presses against each one of my individual ribs. *Am I missing something? Have I missed out on something?*

Luca knocks me with his shoulder, even though we're still sitting close enough that I feel the warmth of his knee against mine. "You're far away again." I feel his breath against my cheek. He squeezes my knee. "Tell me what's on your mind."

"It's nothing," I lie, getting to my feet, nearly tripping over his minefield of computer equipment. His hand falls away, his fingers landing on his bedsheets. "I'm hungry, so I'm going to go get some food." That part is true at least. "Did you eat something?"

Luca nods. "Earlier," he says. "When I was waiting for you. But I'll grab one of my mom's pizzelles and we can talk—"

"There's nothing to talk about." I spin on my heel and leave the room to walk down the hall.

"Is this about Nathaniel?"

Luca's question makes my palsied left foot snag on the floor.

"What?" I spin around, causing a muscle spasm to course down my leg. Luca doesn't know that I saw Nathaniel at the bookstore, or that we actually had our first decent conversation, or that he kissed me goodbye.

"Do you actually have feelings for him?" Luca's brow crinkles as he moves closer to me, the floor creaking beneath him. "Is that why you're not talking to me?"

"What? No." I shake my head. "I don't have feelings for Nathaniel. Don't be ridiculous."

"But it's not ridiculous," Luca presses, taking another step forward. *Creak*. "You argue all the time. Do you actually hate him that much? Or is there something more?"

"We want the same thing." I continue toward the opened front door, Luca still following my footsteps. "That's all."

"If that's all it is, then . . ." Luca's voice fades in his throat, and he pushes his glasses farther up his nose. "Joy, why won't you stay here?"

"Because I'm hungry," I murmur, grateful that my stomach chooses that exact moment to gurgle. "If you need me, you know where I live."

I'm expecting Luca to say something else, to insist I stay.

But he doesn't say anything.

I don't hear the creak of floorboards, either, as I leave his apartment. He didn't even move from his spot.

Even after I've eaten chicken Parm and a piece of chocolate-raspberry Christmas tree cake, I can't stop thinking about Valentina and Yasmine. Or Luca and Hanna.

I've never thought about relationships like this before. As I hug my moms goodnight and get Pomegranate situated in her cat tree before putting on my pajamas, I start to wonder what it would feel like to hold someone's hand, to laugh at a joke that's not even that funny just because you like the person who told it, to sit shoulder to shoulder on the subway even when it's hot, just to be close to that person.

I don't have any answers. And I'm not someone usually without them.

Once I'm in bed, I snuggle against my reading pillow as the gold city light trickles through my window. I know it's late and I should get some sleep. Maybe a new morning will help me think more clearly, let me compartmentalize my thoughts with logic instead of squirrelly emotions.

But instead, I slide my glasses back on and open Instagram again. Navigating over to Valentina's profile, I click on the hashtag for Caldwell Cupid. Dozens of results pop up, more than I can read. Collections of selfies celebrating relationships.

Indira Anand and Sebastian Oaks from AP Biology.

Kosuke Himura and Amir Johnson from AP World History.

Cora Acardi and Maria Garza Villa, from the basketball team.

I scroll down farther to find that some people have actually posted the love letters that Caldwell Cupid wrote for them. And even though it's nearing 1:00 a.m. now, I stop to read all of them:

Dear Christen,
We've been friends for so long, but I want to be more, with no one else but you . . .

Dear Morgan,
I could watch you paint for the rest of my days . . .

Dear Dylan,
You might be going away to Berkley soon, so I know if I don't confess my true feelings now, I might not have the chance . . .

Dear Tia,
I regret that I didn't ask you to junior prom and have spent all summer thinking about how to make it up to you . . .

These are the kinds of love letters I'd like to receive myself.

That thought makes a shiver travel from the tips of my toes to the crown of my head.

Before I can chicken out, I go to Caldwell Cupid's website, composed of a simple purple background and silver text boxes with an invitation to email them in the center.

And with the noises of Union Square as my soundtrack, I start typing.

To: Caldwell Cupid (cupid@caldwellcupid.com)

From: Joy Corvi (joy.corvi@caldwell.edu)

Date: December 25, 3:00 a.m.

Subject: Question

Dear Cupid,

Is there a formula for romance?

Sincerely,

Joy

CHAPTER SEVEN
CALDWELL CUPID

"Is there a formula for romance?"

The question stares back at me from my computer screen, the letters searing my eyes.

But it's not the question that's puzzling me.

It's the person who asked it.

Joy Corvi. Quiet, academically minded Joy.

"If you keep making that face, it'll get stuck that way," Franny says from my bedroom doorway, snapping me back to earth.

"Isn't that just a myth?" I minimize the email, pushing away from my desk. Like, if I don't see Joy's question, I won't need to think about it.

"Perhaps." Franny shrugs, smirking at me. "But something has you thinking hard enough to make a face. What's up?"

Franny is the one person I tell everything to. But for some reason, I don't want to talk to her about this.

"It's nothing." I get to my feet, twisting my waist. "Just school."

"How about this?" Franny pats her rounded stomach, running her finger along her red cable-knit sweater. "Baby and I are getting hungry. Take a break and help me make lunch? I'm thinking BLTs."

"Sure." I breathe a sigh of relief and follow her down to the kitchen.

We fall into a rhythm; I toast the bread and wash the lettuce while Franny slices up tomatoes and checks the bacon as it finishes cooking. We don't talk—the sound of us moving around the kitchen is enough noise for us. It's nice to just be quiet, without much of a thought in my head.

"So." Franny plops two red plates onto the dining room table—an old farmhouse piece our grandfather built for our grandmother as a wedding present—and turns to me. "Who's on your mind?"

I nearly choke on a mouthful of bacon and lettuce. "Excuse me?" I ask, pounding my chest with my fist.

"You heard me," Franny says, unceremoniously smacking my back. "Who's on your mind?" Her eyes brighten, and she scoots closer in her seat. "What's their name?"

"I don't have anyone on my mind," I lie, taking my first full bite of lunch. The bacon is perfectly crisp, the tomatoes are thin, and my sister's suggestion to swap out mayo for garlic aioli has changed my life from this point forward. "Just . . . school."

Franny tuts. "You know," she says, "senior year can be stressful, but I know that look and it's not over some schoolwork. Honestly, if you have *someone*—"

Before she can finish that sentence, there's a knock on the door.

Saving myself from being lectured by my sister, I spring to my feet and walk down the hallway.

Who could be at our door on Christmas Day? Both Everett and Warren are working, so who—

When I undo the locks and pull the door open, I have my answer.

"Joy?" My mouth falls open just slightly at the image of her standing at the top of my stoop, dressed in jeans and a purple coat with her ace pride flag wrapped around her throat. "What are you doing here?"

"Hi, Nathaniel," she murmurs, her cheeks flushed from the cold. "Did you forget that you invited me over?"

CHAPTER EIGHT
JOY

Nathaniel lives in a brownstone in the Upper West Side. So, I'm braving the NYC public transportation system on Christmas. For him. It was a disaster trying to get out of the apartment this morning. My moms were aghast at the thought of me spending Christmas Day with Nathaniel.

"Nathaniel?" Momma kept asking.

"The guy you've been competing against for the last three years?" Ma kept saying. "The arrogant one who's always got you raging about one thing or the other? That same Nathaniel?"

"It's just to . . . prepare stuff for the science club," I said, as if that made the very idea of visiting his house any less weird. "Can I go? Is that okay? I didn't think it would be a big deal; we don't really celebrate today."

My moms exchanged a look with each other. The kind

of glance that's actually a whole conversation without words.

"Well, that's not why it's a big deal," Ma muttered under her breath.

"Don't be too late," Momma said.

"And you're not going over there empty-handed, Joy," Ma added, gesturing to the serving hatch. "The leftover rainbow cookies are in a Tupperware in the fridge. Bring those."

When I reach Nathaniel's brownstone on West Eighty-Ninth Street, a thought weasels its way into my brain before I can ring the doorbell: *Will there be other people here? Am I going to have to explain cerebral palsy? Will they view me as some sort of medical oddity and ask me questions?*

The door opens, putting an end to my anxious internal monologue, revealing Nathaniel standing at the threshold. His deep green turtleneck clings to his chest; his dark-wash jeans reveal how slim his hips are. I'm horrified to find both things kind of attractive on him. (Another thing I will never tell my friends.)

But I doubt I'm having the same effect on Nathaniel, especially because of the way his eyes have slightly narrowed.

"Joy?" he asks. "What are you doing here?"

"Hi, Nathaniel," I murmur. "Did you forget that you invited me over?"

Before he can answer, a beautiful pregnant woman with long gold hair and blue eyes, dressed in black yoga pants and a cute red cable-knit sweater, bustles over to us.

"Hi!" she says cheerily. "Happy holidays! I'm Francine." She turns to Nathaniel, her curtain of silky hair smacking her shoulder. "You have a girlfriend, and you didn't tell me?"

A what? My heart lodges itself in my throat.

Hoping that I can figure out what to say, I open my mouth, but Nathaniel beats me to it. "Franny." He has the same groan in his voice now that he does for me. "Joy is *not* my girlfriend."

"She's a girl," Francine says, "and she's your friend, right?"

"What are you, twelve years old?" Nathaniel replies dryly. "Shouldn't you be sitting down?"

"Please." She laughs, placing a hand on her swollen stomach. "I'm allowed to walk around."

"Walking can stimulate labor," Nathaniel rattles off as though he'd just swallowed an entire textbook on obstetrics. "Mother would kill me if she knew you weren't on the couch." He gestures off to the side. "Please."

Francine clucks her tongue. "All right," she says. "Fine. I'll go sit down. But a few things first." She holds up a finger with an expertly done French tip, narrowing her own eyes as she smirks. If I had any doubts that she and Nathaniel were related, they're gone now. "Pregnant people walk literally all the time, and babies don't come shooting out of them. And," she continues, "I'm a pediatrician. If my daughter were to come out of me right now, I'd know what to do with her." She pokes his sweater, her smirk widening as one unfurls across his face. "You need to stop worryin' and stressin' like you are. It's not good for your body."

"If Mother and Father were here, they'd be telling you the same thing," Nathaniel replies as Francine makes her way to the living room. He turns his full attention toward me for the first time since I've showed up.

"Hi," I say, to fill the sudden silence if nothing else.

"Hi." Nathaniel puts his hands into his jeans pockets.

"I, uh, brought rainbow cookies." I hold up the Tupperware.

Nathaniel gives me a quizzical look as the TV is turned on in the living room. "What are they?" he asks.

"You've never had rainbow cookies?" I ask, my eyes wide. "They're layers of dyed almond sponge cake filled with raspberry jam and covered in chocolate," I explain as his eyes slowly begin to match mine. "C'mon, we can eat them as we work."

"Do you mind if we work in the living room?" Nathaniel asks, stepping in front of the staircase.

"Sure," I say. "No problem."

"For heaven's sake!" Francine crows, muting the TV. "I'm pregnant, that's all. I can look after myself."

"I don't want to get an earful from Mother when she gets back home," Nathaniel tells her.

As I hang up my coat, scarf, and gloves in the hall closet, storing my sneakers just below, I realize that I haven't heard a single noise beyond our conversation, as awkward as it has been.

"Everyone in my family is a doctor," Nathaniel explains. "It's not like hospitals close for Christmas."

"My mom was lucky she got the day off," I say, nodding.

"I'm the odd one out." Francine chuckles from the oatmeal-colored armchair angled off to the side, her feet propped up on a matching ottoman. "I'm here to bother this one all day long." She winks at Nathaniel, who gives a small smile back as we sit down on the oatmeal-colored couch. In addition to cream walls; polished wood floors; a massive, crackling fireplace; a towering Christmas tree filled with a popcorn-and-cranberry garland; a canvas photograph of a sunset on a beach; and a huge flat-screen TV, there are two huge windows that overlook West Eighty-Ninth Street.

It's a place as cozy as my own, somewhere I didn't expect Nathaniel to live. I was envisioning someplace cold and gray, something severely modern with no personal touches.

"What is that smell?" Francine says, sniffing the air.

"Rainbow cookies," I say, offering the Tupperware to her. "Here, try them."

Francine plucks one of the tiny square cookies from the box. Holding it between her thumb and forefinger, she examines the delicate layers of pink, green, and yellow cake before popping it into her mouth. "Holy shit." She groans, immediately snatching up another one. "They're so good! Nathaniel, here." She holds out the Tupperware. "Have one before I eat them all."

"I'll eat later." Nathaniel positions a shiny MacBook Pro on his lap, opening it up. "Did you bring your computer, Joy?" he asks without looking at me.

"No—" I start to say, unsure of how to explain that I was so distracted that I forgot to bring my laptop.

"She brought food." Francine rubs her sweater, smiling gently. "Baby is kicking, so she likes the cookies, too. Plus, you don't need a computer to study."

Nathaniel looks at his sister over the edge of his laptop. "Since you have such a strong opinion, do you have any ideas for activities?"

"Nope." Francine pops another rainbow cookie into her mouth as Nathaniel takes one from the box. "I'm merely here for moral support." As if her smile pulls him away, Nathaniel practically anchors himself to the arm on the opposite end of the couch. He holds the rainbow cookie between his fingers, the chocolate just beginning to melt down them.

"Eat," I say. "Eat it. You don't want it to melt more."

Instead of popping the whole cookie into his mouth like his sister, Nathaniel eats half. He chews it thoughtfully, angling his head up to the tall ceiling.

"It's delicious," he says, his Adam's apple bobbing as he swallows. His eyes slide over to mine. "It was strangely nice of you to bring cookies."

I lean back against the couch, taking a rainbow cookie from the Tupperware. "What do you mean?" I ask, eating the whole tiny square in one bite.

"You don't like me. You make that very clear all the time," he replies. "You're trying to get me to let my guard down, aren't you? So you can win the bet!"

"Why—Why would you"—my entire left arm tightens in a muscle spasm, my fist dipping into his couch cushions—"think that?"

"I'm just making sure you remember our bet," Nathaniel says.

"Of course I do," I reply coolly. Suddenly any notion of how good he looks in that sweater and those jeans is gone.

"You can't charm me with sweets, Joy."

"My mom made me bring them, you pompous ass," I retort. "I was being polite."

"Well, that's new." Nathaniel spreads both of his arms.

"What is *wrong* with you, Nathaniel?" Francine asks from her armchair. Her voice is no longer sugary sweet, but stern. "Don't be mean to your girlfriend like that."

"Franny, she's not my—" Nathaniel begins, but I cut him off by getting to my feet.

"I'm not his girlfriend," I say, turning on my right heel. (Lord knows if I turned on my left, I'd fall into the Wrights' coffee table and need Francine to tend to my injuries.) "We're not even friends. We just run a science club together." Squaring my shoulders and biting my cheek, I look at Nathaniel. It's a marvel how his sister has only just met me and has been nicer to me than he ever has, a realization that makes tears prick at my eyes.

I leave the living room and gather my things from the hall closet. As I'm buttoning up my coat, I hear Francine tersely whispering to Nathaniel about something I only make out about half of:

"Why did you do that?" she hisses. "I've never seen you like this."

"It's complicated," Nathaniel replies, his voice low. "Never mind. You don't need to worry about me."

"Just as you—"

After slipping into my sneakers, I walk out the front door, closing it behind me and blocking out the rest of their conversation. My body immediately starts to seize from the cold, so I take my time walking down the steps to the street, swiping at the tears that roll down my cheeks.

And by the time I've reached the sidewalk, the door opens again from behind me.

"Joy." Though not malicious, Nathaniel's voice is loud in my ears, despite the distance between us. "Can I—"

"Can you what?" I whirl around, glaring up the stairs at him. My frustration has melted away. Anger now pumps through my bloodstream as its replacement. "Talk to me? Be an asshole again?" My left hand curls into a fist, my arm jerkily rising until it's level with my breasts.

Nathaniel's shoulders slump, a motion that looks so out of character on someone who carries himself so tall and confident.

"Why were you so nice to me on Christmas Eve? Why did you kiss me goodbye?" I shout the question that's been on my mind ever since.

"I—it's hard to say," Nathaniel says quietly.

"Really?" I hiss. "You can humiliate me in front of other people, but can't tell me that?"

"No." Nathaniel squares his shoulders, clearing his throat. "Joy, I can't."

I turn on my right heel and walk away from his brownstone, trying to convince myself that the new batch of tears welling up in my eyes is from the cold.

DECEMBER 26

Joy (11:00 a.m.): Can we hang out? I need to tell you something.

Valentina (11:05 a.m.): Really?! Is it gossip?

Yasmine (11:06 a.m.): Luca's gonna be upset he's upstate! 😊

Joy (11:10 a.m.): Can we get fondue at Max Brenner's? 🍫😋

Yasmine (11:12 a.m.): Meet in the lobby in 10 minutes! 🙂

CHAPTER NINE
JOY

Yasmine and Valentina wait until our chocolate fondue—accompanied by marshmallows, strawberries, bananas, cookies, sponge cake, and toffee sauce—arrives before they share a glance with each other in their booth.

"So." Valentina plucks a marshmallow and sticks it onto a metal skewer. She dangles it over the miniature firepit on the table, letting the marshmallow get bubbly and crisp. "What do you need to tell us?"

Yasmine and I each select a strawberry, dipping them both in the milk chocolate fondue. "Well." I hold my skewer in front of my mouth instead of actually eating what's on it. "Something happened on Christmas Eve."

"Oh my God," Yasmine says, her voice hushed.

"At the party? With Luca?" Valentine pushes her glasses farther up on the bridge of her nose. "Did he . . . ?" She glances at Yasmine, her eyes wide, before turning back to me. "Joy, did he *kiss* you?"

"What?" I scrunch up my face before sticking my strawberry into my mouth and pulling it off the skewer. Yasmine grabs her skewer from the fondue pot, eating the strawberry. The glass cases filled with blocks of milk, white, and dark chocolate behind her and Valentina gleam beneath Max Brenner's honey-colored lights. "W-Why would Luca kiss me? What are you talking about?" I take a sip of ice water.

"Joy." Valentina dips her marshmallow into the fondue and eats it. "Because he *likes* you?"

"Of course he likes me," I say. With my strawberry eaten, I select a marshmallow next and hold it over the firepit. "But just as friends."

Yasmine dunks a piece of sponge cake into the fondue. "Then why does he put his arm around you all the time?"

I shrug, my left hand becoming spastic on the knee of my jeans. "W-We've been friends for so long," I say. "So, we hug. That's all."

Valentina puts a piece of banana on her skewer and dips it into the fondue. "Did you do the thing where everyone is having a party in your apartments, but you and Luca hung out in his room the whole time?"

"Well, not the whole time." I study my marshmallow as it toasts. "But that's what we always do."

"Think about it." Valentine grins at me. "Christmas Eve. The music. The ambiance. The alone time. Just the two of you. Don't you think that's kind of . . . sexy?"

It's my turn to drop my skewer. I scramble to pick it up because I like my marshmallows toasty and gooey. "I don't care about what's *sexy* to *Luca*," I say, laughing again. "Or anyone."

"Mostly? Same." Valentina pushes back the sleeves of her chunky star-patterned cardigan, revealing her pride bracelets. On her right hand, a lesbian one. On her left, an ace one. She came out as gray ace around the same time I came out as ace last year. "My girlfriend, though?" She turns to Yasmine, grinning and giving her a kiss.

"Our point is." Yasmine kisses Valentina back, both of them turning to face me. "Maybe he does like you. Like in a romantic kind of way?"

"That's not what's happening here."

"You think that." Valentina's eyes gleam as she fixes her cardigan sleeves. "But also consider this: Scene, interior, Luca's living room on Christmas Eve. The tree is all lit up."

"Christmas music is playing," Yasmine continues dreamily. "With the Yule log channel on Netflix for added flair."

"Babe!" Valentina takes a sip of water, clapping her hands. "Thank you! Anyway, so it's just the two of you. Luca leans over and says something completely cheesy like"—she takes a second to clear her throat, to perfect Luca's voice, which is only slightly lower than hers—"*'Joy, the only gift I want isn't under the Christmas tree'!*"

"Yes!" Yasmine cheers, bouncing up and down in her seat, the upholstery squeaking against her jeans. "Yes, yes! And then he pulls you to him and the two of you *make out* as the music swells!"

My friends look at me from across the table before bursting into giggles.

"No." I take a bite of my marshmallow. "That will absolutely not happen."

"In our minds, it does!" Valentina sings, using her piece of chocolate-covered banana as a microphone.

I blink at my friends. "No," I say finally. "The two of you are so in love that you're seeing prospective couples everywhere. And now you think everyone likes everyone else. Luca and I are not into each other like that."

"Okay, maybe you aren't." Yasmine smiles, eating another piece of sponge cake. "But he is definitely into you."

Valentina nudges her with her shoulder. "Maybe we shouldn't say any more."

"What?" Yasmine says. "I just want everyone to be happy!"

"I know," I say. "But I-I'm happy right now. Believe me," I continue, rambling. "I-I'll win valedictorian, start nursing school, and *then* I will meet someone to fall in love with."

"You have a plan." Yasmine grins. "Good!"

"Speaking of plans." Valentina takes another sip of water. "Have we made New Year's Eve plans?"

"We are *not* going to the ball drop," Yasmine says. "No, thank you."

"That's not what I have in mind." Valentina chuckles. "How about we all get dressed up, come over to my apartment, and watch the ball drop on TV? My parents are going to my tía's, Carlos is going to a friend's, and Daniel is working. The place will be ours. Luca can come, too."

"Sure," I say.

"Sounds perfect," Yasmine adds.

"I thought so." Valentina grins.

We finish our fondue and walk back to our apartment building in the beginnings of a snowstorm. We all practically run for the elevator, like the closer we are to our individual units, the warmer we'll become.

"Are you guys okay?" I ask as we all press the numbers for our floors.

"Yeah," Valentina says. "Just cold and snowy."

"You have snowflakes in your hair," Yasmine giggles.

"We all have snowflakes in our hair, babe." Valentina snuggles into Yasmine's puffy coat, and Yasmine leans her cheeks on top of her head.

"Well, yeah," she murmurs, smiling softly. "But the ones in your hair are cute."

When the elevator doors ding open on the seventeenth floor, I hug Valentina and Yasmine before walking down the hallway to my unit, my sneakers squeaking with each step.

"Welcome home, baby!" Momma meets me at the door. "Get in the shower," she says as I put my things in the closet. "You'll catch your death in all these cold clothes. Your ma will be home round seven. Does takeout from Café Istanbul sound good? They started doing delivery again, now that Sabah's son and his fiancée have moved back from California."

Even though it's full of chocolate, fruit, and marshmallows, my stomach growls in anticipation. Since both my moms work long hours, we order takeout more than we cook.

I nod. "Sounds delicious. Can we get some fırın sütlaç for dessert?"

Momma raises a red eyebrow, but she's smiling. "Didn't you just have fondue with your friends?" she asks, chuckling. "You have a sweet tooth bigger than mine. We'll see what Ma wants, okay?"

"All right." I step out of my sneakers and store them in the closet.

After a hot shower that soothes my spastic muscles, I dress in a pair of black leggings and an oversized purple sweater that droops off one shoulder. And by the time I burrow into my blankets for extra coziness, my phone lights up with a notification:

I have a new email. From Caldwell Cupid. They wrote me back.

To: Joy Corvi (joy.corvi@caldwell.edu)
From: Caldwell Cupid (cupid@caldwellcupid.com)
Date: December 26, 11:30 a.m.
Subject: RE: Question

Dear Joy,
I'm sorry for taking a few days to write back to you. But your question made me think.

I don't think there's a formula for romance, exactly. Everyone's experience with it is different. And if there were a singular formula for romance, we'd all have the same kind of experience, right?

But I will tell you this: I get my inspiration for letters from other love stories. Plays, movies, novels. Everything.

Based on my research I can only assume that the closest thing to a formula for love is . . . a trope.
Best of luck,
Caldwell Cupid 💘

P.S. Why do you ask? People write to me with love letter requests, but no one has ever asked me a question.

To: Caldwell Cupid (cupid@caldwellcupid.com)

From: Joy Corvi (joy.corvi@caldwell.edu)

Date: December 26, 2:31 p.m.

Subject: RE: RE: Question

Dear Cupid,

I wrote to you because I'm graduating in June, which is just a few months away. And I've realized something about myself:

I've missed out on having a romantic relationship in high school. I know not everyone under the asexual umbrella wants romance, but seeing my friends fall in love has made me realize that I might want that, too. Maybe it's just the anxiety of it all, but I'm starting to wonder . . . If I don't fall in love with someone before graduation, will I ever?

Since you read a lot, can you tell me about your favorite tropes? Maybe I can use them to find romance?

Sincerely,

Joy

CHAPTER TEN

JOY

It's been five days since I wrote back to Caldwell Cupid. I haven't received a reply from them yet; thank goodness I have our New Year's Eve Extravaganza (Luca's name, not mine) to distract me.

At least, I will when I manage to get the back of this rose-gold dress zipped up. As a disabled person, I normally stay away from dresses with zippers in the back—or complicated jeans with more than one button—but this dress, with its delicate sequins, was too cute to leave behind.

Plus, it fits me perfectly. Which is a rarity when you're both short and fat. Just to be clear, I like my body. It's clothing companies that don't.

"Shit," I breathe, hopping up and down in the middle of my room. Our other cat, an orange tabby with cerebellar hypoplasia named Lasagna, runs into the hallway.

I'm home alone, so I don't have anyone to help me. I'll need to get into the elevator with the back of my dress open. Maybe because it's New Year's Eve the elevator will be empty? Maybe if I run fast enough that can happen? What other choice do I have?

I could just pick something else, but this dress is the only one I own with sequins. It basically screams New Year's Eve party.

I let out another frustrated huff, but strap on my Mary Janes and hurry out of my apartment. When I reach the hallway, anxiety pumps through my veins alongside the blood.

But the combination of that and the running has made my leg muscles seize up, rooting me to the tile floor.

"C'mon," I hiss, massaging them through my opaque black tights. "Not now. Hurry up." I sag against the door, closing my eyes.

"Joy?" a woman's voice asks a moment later. "Are you okay?"

"Yeah." I sigh, opening my eyes. My neighbors Daisy and Noah have just stepped into the hallway next to me with their daughter, Luisa, situated in her car seat. They're all dressed in black with gold accents. Even the tulle in Luisa's tutu peeking out from her puffy pink teddy bear winter coat shimmers like her parents' gold wedding rings.

"It's just a muscle spasm," I explain. "I've, um. Been trying to zip up my dress?"

"Let me help." Daisy's lips scrunch up and her brow furrows. She has cerebral palsy, too, so she knows all about what my legs feel like now—and how impossible doing things behind our backs is for us. "Turn around." She motions with her right hand, and I spin on my heel.

"It's been a while since I've seen you guys," I say, awkwardly facing the wall.

"It has," Noah replies. "We've just been so busy."

"We have," Daisy agrees. "Especially since Luisa was born. But we wouldn't have it any other way." She pauses as she zips up the dress. "There you go, Joy."

"Thank you," I say gratefully once I'm facing her again.

"You're welcome." Daisy smiles.

"Be safe and have fun tonight, okay?" Noah adjusts his glasses with the hand not holding the car seat handle. Luisa babbles up at me happily, her eyes wide behind her own glasses.

"You too," I reply, pushing my own tortoiseshell glasses farther up the bridge of my nose. "Happy New Year!"

When I arrive at Valentina's, we all gather in the living room. It's home to comfortable leather couches, a basket of her mom's hand-knit throw blankets, and clusters of family photographs on the walls. Valentina's quinceañera; family trips to Mexico City; her parents' wedding photo, where they're gazing at each other the same way they do now; and more.

"Okay!" Valentina sings, placing a pizza box and container

of garlic knots on the coffee table. She dances, the skirt of her electric-blue beaded dress twirling as she moves.

"Let the New Year's Eve Extravaganza begin!" Yasmine says, looking incredible in a knee-length purple dress. "And by that," she adds, "I mean, let's eat."

We cheers with our red Solo cups of strawberry lemonade. When Yasmine opens the pizza box, my stomach grumbles at the delicious, greasy smell of chicken, bacon, ranch, and cheese that wafts around the room.

"How was upstate, Luca?" Valentina asks.

Luca swallows his mouthful of pizza and sighs, leaning back against the couch. "It was fine," he says, his pizza's cheese pull dangling way too close to his fuchsia tuxedo. "A little lonely."

"Lonely?" I repeat, taking a bite of pizza. "How? Your family is huge. There are always people around."

"Yeah, but I missed you." Luca settles against my shoulder, his sequins itching my bare skin as sweat springs to life on my back.

"Well, we're together now." Yasmine smiles, folding her pizza slice in half. "Like we always have been and always will be," she says in mock seriousness.

"Um." The simple word—only two letters, only one syllable—breaks apart in my mouth. I don't know why I said it, but all eyes shifted to me. I can't chicken out now. "A-Actually, we won't be. Together."

"What?" Yasmine and Valentina whirl to face me, their brows crinkled. "Why?"

"W-Well." Placing my paper plate onto the coffee table, I fold my hands in front of me. My left hand scrabbles at the back of my right. I take a deep breath, one big enough to physically hurt as my lungs expand in my chest. "I got accepted to the Clara Barton School of Nursing at the California Institute of Biology."

"You got into CIB?!" Valentina gasps. She throws her arms around me, knocking Luca's away. "Joy! That's incredible! They only accept *five* percent of applicants! I'm so proud of you!"

I smile into her shoulder, relief coursing through my bloodstream. "Thank you," I say against her dress.

"We should've expected you to get into one of the best nursing programs in the country!" Yasmine's arms come around me next. "Congratulations!"

"My ma went to CIB," I explain. "I-I'm really excited—"

"Excited?" Luca repeats. The word drips from his mouth, and he stares forward instead of turning toward us. "You're not actually thinking of going? Why?"

"Wh-What are you talking about?" I ask him as Valentina and Yasmine disentangle themselves to sit back down on the couch. "Why wouldn't I go? Why shouldn't I be excited?"

"Because, Joy." Luca's eyes finally slide to mine. I once thought they were the warm brown of his mom's hot chocolate.

Now, they're more like the crumpled fall leaves buried under the snow outside. Cold. "You're *leaving* us. You're leaving us after graduation, and it's like you don't even care."

Luca's words send a chill over the living room, as if the winter has managed to seep through the windows.

"Luca." Valentina turns to him. "You don't need to be a dick."

"But I'm not, Val," Luca splutters. His defensiveness makes my stomach clench. "It's the truth. We're all staying here, and Joy's going across the country. She's leaving us. And she lied." He sighs, shoving his hand through his brown hair. "Early decisions went out, what, the week before break? She must've known about her acceptance to CIB for *over a week*. Didn't you, Joy?"

I open my mouth to say something—anything; it doesn't even have to be a witty, snarky retort—but instead, air just passes over my tongue.

"I-I—" My voice has shrunk, and my eyes focus on my folded hands because I can't bring myself to look at my friends. "Yes. I did."

"So she didn't tell us right away; you don't have to be rude to her about it," Yasmine says.

"Friends . . ." Valentina adds, her voice tight. ". . . going to different states for colleges is normal." She wipes at her lower eyelids with her thumb. "It-It's just a thing that happens, you know?"

"I-I'm sorry." The apology dissolves into tears in my mouth. "But we—we can stay in touch, and I'll be back for Christmas."

Even so, a hollow ache forms in my stomach, widening with each passing second as if, despite how relieved I am to have finally told my friends, I'm getting an ulcer anyway.

"We know," Yasmine whispers.

"And we know what a big opportunity this is for you, too." Valentina sniffles as she, Yasmine, and I wipe tears from our cheeks. "You deserve it!"

"Are you really sorry, Joy?" Luca asks.

"Luca." I turn to him, my left leg locking up into a muscle spasm again. "I know this is going to be hard."

He laughs humorlessly, placing his plate of pizza on the coffee table. "I can't believe you."

"You know what?" I burst out. "Y-You can be upset, angry, whatever you want to be with me right now."

"Good." Luca drags his free hand through his hair again. "Because I'm both of those things. I'm upset and angry that you're leaving us. And I'm upset and angry that you didn't tell us this until now. It's like my opinion doesn't matter—"

"Wait." The fingers on my left hand chew into my palm. *"Your opinion?"*

"You don't actually think that Joy needs to consider your opinion about her own future?" Yasmine asks, rubbing her girlfriend's back.

"Yeah, it's her life. She doesn't owe anyone that," Valentina agrees.

He sighs, adjusting his glasses. "Joy, we've been best friends since we were six years old. We've always been there for each other."

"And we still can be," I murmur, reaching for him. Luca closes his hands around mine, his grip reassuring—his touch, his pulse beneath his fingers telling me what we both know. "I'll just . . ." My voice trails off, my wet lashes brushing against my face.

"Be across the country," Luca whispers, his own words thick with tears now, too. "And that's what you want?"

"You know how important this is to me," I tell him, as if he doesn't already know this. "CIB is a huge opportunity; I'd be foolish to turn it down."

"No." Luca slips his hands away from mine, and I already miss his warmth. The clouded look in his eyes is so different from how he usually looks at me. Now I wonder if Valentina and Yasmine were onto something. "Even if it means leaving me? Us?"

"I don't *want* to leave you, but its CIB! I *have* to do this," I tell him feebly.

"No, Joy, you don't have to do this."

"Okay, you're right," I say. "But I want to."

Luca rises to his feet, the fuchsia sequins sparkling as he fixes his tux's suit jacket.

"I can't be here right now," he says.

"You know what you're doing, Luca?" Valentina asks, wrapping her arm around me. "You're making Joy's future about you. It's hers before it's anyone else's."

"Until now, our futures have always included one another," Luca retorts. "Always. We had a plan, and it's like she doesn't care about it."

"Of course she cares," Yasmine tells him. "If you'd stop being a selfish asshole and actually be her friend, you'd see that."

"Oh my God." Luca scrubs his hands over his face. "I'm selfish? Joy's the one—Never mind." He shakes his head. "I'll see you at school."

He leaves without another word, slamming the heavy apartment door behind him.

"Sorry about him," I find myself saying, looking between Yasmine and Valentina.

"Why?" Valentina murmurs, squeezing my shoulder.

"He should be the one apologizing to you." Yasmine hugs me from my other side.

"Don't think about him anymore tonight." Valentina gives me a quick hug, then reaches for another slice of pizza. "Let's be productive instead and talk about our *new* plans."

"Great idea." Yasmine lets go of me to take another sip of strawberry lemonade. "A nurse, an exercise physiologist, and a science teacher." She smiles. "Three queer women in STEM."

"I *love* that." I grin back at her.

"And us?" Valentina kisses Yasmine's cheek. "We're gonna be such a nerdy power couple!"

"Aren't we already, though?" Yasmine gives her a kiss, leaning her forehead against Valentina's for a second. She looks over at me. "Are you still set on finding someone and getting your happily ever after with them, Joy?"

I laugh, choking on my strawberry lemonade. "Very funny," I say.

"Hey." Valentina chuckles, knocking her red Solo cup into mine. "Don't completely rule it out."

"Fine." I sigh, smirking. I'd be lying if I said joking around like this didn't provide me with such welcome relief. "I'll let the experiment be carried out. Happy?"

"Very," my best friends say in unison before dissolving into giggles.

To: Caldwell Cupid (cupid@caldwellcupid.com)
From: Anonymous (anonymouscaldwell@mailthis.com)
Date: December 31, 10:10 p.m.
Subject: Joy

Dear Cupid,

Her name is Joy. There are so many things I love about her. She's smart, she's reliable.

And I thought she would always be there.

It's probably foolish, I know, but that's what I always expected. We've been together for over a decade, so why would she want that to change after high school?

Joy is going to the California Institute of Biology in the fall. She is moving across the country.

She's leaving me.

And I know I can't stop her.

I respect Joy, of course I do, but that doesn't mean that I'm not upset with her for leaving.

Luca

To: Anonymous (anonymouscaldwell@mailthis.com)

From: Caldwell Cupid (cupid@caldwellcupid.com)

Date: December 31, 10:33 p.m.

Subject: RE: Joy

Dear Luca,

If you really respected Joy, here's what you would do instead:

(Saved to drafts)

To: Joy Corvi (joy.corvi@caldwell.edu)

From: Caldwell Cupid (cupid@caldwellcupid.com)

Date: January 1, 12:00 p.m.

Subject: My Favorite Tropes

Dear Joy,

It's never too late! These are some of my favorite tropes, in no particular order:

- **The meet-cute:** Where a couple meets for the first time in a cute, unexpected way. Think bumping into each other in the hallway or even sitting next to them on the subway.
- **Rivals to lovers:** This one is self-explanatory. But God, what a setup! There's so much passion and history with this one. Why are they rivals? There's an undercurrent of unconscious respect here too, so that just adds to everything!
- **Mistaken or withheld identity:** This is where one person knows another person's identity, but the other doesn't. Or they think they are falling for one person, but it's really someone else.
- **Forced proximity:** This one is where something is forcing two characters to be together. And it's that closeness—that proximity—that causes them to develop feelings.

I guess you could say I'm a big emotions type of reader.

And love letter crafter? I like to think of it as practice for writing my own romance novels.

So, my advice is to take these tropes to heart and see what you can make of them.

Best of luck,

Caldwell Cupid ❤

January 2nd

Nathaniel (7:00 a.m.): Joy? Can you meet me before class?

Joy (7:02 a.m.): Why?

Nathaniel (7:05 a.m.): I just need to talk, to apologize for how we left things at my house on Christmas.

Joy (7:05 a.m.): Do you need to? Or do you want to? Because there is a difference.

Nathaniel (7:07 a.m.): I want to.

Joy (7:07 a.m.): Okay then. Let's meet by your locker.

CHAPTER ELEVEN

~~CALDWELL CUPID~~

NATHANIEL

I walk to my locker the next morning practicing what I am going to say to Joy. I am so focused I don't hear Declan and Vikram's debate about the best romance anime coming out this season. Their voices are a low hum beside me as I walk right into something.

Someone.

"Ow!" Joy grumbles from the floor. She scowls up at me, and my heart clenches. *What a great start to my apology.* "Can you be more careful, please?"

"I'm so sorry!" My hands fly to my mouth, embarrassment pricking my spine. "I didn't mean to knock you down. Are you okay?"

"Yeah." She looks over to the side, her left hand clenching on her knees. "I'm fine. Just give me a minute."

"Nathaniel," Declan says. "Maybe you should help her up?"

"Um." I drop my hands. "I would, but, Joy, isn't there a rule about doing things for disabled people without asking them?"

Joy whips her head to face me, her eyes wide behind her tortoiseshell glasses. "There is," she says, now lying back on both of her hands.

"I just don't want to overstep—" I splutter.

"You asked." Joy blows at her bangs. "You can help me up. If you want."

I bend down and take Joy's hand in mine, threading my fingers through hers. A chill runs up my arm as I pull her to her feet.

"Well!" Vikram stretches his arms above his head. "I'm going to go meet Yasmine before class. Cheerleading competition prep stuff. Bye!" He turns on his heel and starts walking away from us.

"And I!" Declan places both hands on his chest, projecting his voice as he walks backward. "Well, I think today might be the day when those therapy dogs are coming to relieve student stress. And I'm not passing up a chance to experience the serotonin only a pile of golden retrievers can provide."

"But that's not until—" Joy and I say in unison.

"Good luck!" my best friends harmonize as they disappear down another hallway.

"Good luck?" Joy raises an eyebrow, adjusting her glasses. "What do they mean?"

"Oh." I swallow around a lump in my throat. Both of us

jolt when we realize that we're still holding hands. "I have it written down. Hang on." Disentangling our fingers and pulling my phone out of my coat pocket, I open up my Notes app.

I clear my throat and begin. "I, Nathaniel Theodore Wright, must formally apologize to you, Joy middle name—" Glancing up from my phone, I find Joy staring at me, her eyes wide. "What's your middle name?"

"Elise," she says, her voice soft.

"Elise," I repeat, testing out the letters on my tongue. She nods, and I turn my phone back around to keep reading.

"I, Nathaniel Theodore Wright, must formally apologize to you, Joy Elise Corvi, for my behavior on Christmas," I restart. "I humbly request your forgiveness with the hope that we can still be academically embroiled until one of us is declared valedictorian in April." I tuck my phone back into my pocket to find that Joy hasn't looked away from me. And for some reason, that makes my stomach swoop. "Oh, and also I'm sorry for barreling into you a moment ago," I ad-lib.

"Oh." Joy's gaze shifts from my face down to her shoes. "Thank you, Nathaniel. I—I accept." The bell dings for first period, and we both look up at the ceiling as if we can see the soft sound. "We should get to class."

"Sure." I fall into step beside Joy, stopping when her left foot snags on the polished tile floor. "Are you all right?" My forehead crumples with concern.

Joy looks up at me again, shaking her head. "Yeah, I'm

fine. Stumbling is just a thing that happens with cerebral palsy."

"No." I shake my head back. "I understand that part."

"You do?" Joy's eyes widen. We both may have blue eyes, but hers are exactly like the ocean.

"Yes," I say.

"Oh."

The reply is so small I barely hear it, even though she and I are closer than we've been since I kissed her cheek on Christmas Eve.

"Does that . . . surprise you?" I murmur. My voice is now as small as hers. Like we're telling secrets.

"Honestly?" Joy hugs herself, her arms pressing against her chest. "Yes. My own pediatrician barely understands cerebral palsy. Why do you?"

"I hate that." I shake my head again, blinking at the spots of light across my vision. "People showing you respect shouldn't be surprising; it should be expected."

"You're right." Joy glances up at the ceiling, blinking quickly.

"Can you look at me?" I whisper. "Please?" The second bell dings, but neither of us moves. Instead, she angles her face toward mine again. "What's wrong? Did something happen?"

I mentally flip through the letters she's written to Caldwell Cupid, hoping to pull any kind of hint of why she might be upset.

"It's nothing," Joy says. "We're already late for AP Biology."

A jolt passes along my spine. "We're never late," I say.

Joy looks off to the side. "First time for everything," she replies quietly as we head toward Mr. Baumann's classroom.

Yes. My heart thrums in my chest, and I can feel it beating in my throat. Bump, bump, bump, bump. *There is.*

"Speaking of," I say as we near Mr. Baumann's door, "would you like to meet in the library after school?"

"The library?" Joy repeats. "Why?"

"Well," I begin sheepishly. "We still need to come up with ideas for the elementary school science night."

"Meeting on neutral ground," Joy murmurs, making my lips quirk upward into a smile. "I like it. Sure."

"Great," I say as Mr. Baumann begins his lesson on heredity. "I'll . . . see you then."

To: Caldwell Cupid (cupid@caldwellcupid.com)

From: Joy Corvi (joy.corvi@caldwell.edu)

Date: January 2, 12:15 p.m.

Subject: Respect

Dear Cupid,

I made a big decision about my future, and I think I may have lost one of my best friends over it. I know the stress of graduation is probably getting to him. And of course, I understand why he is upset. We have been close since we were young. And now that our lives won't be the same in five months? It's scary.

I know Luca is worried about me. He's just not saying it. He wants things to stay the same so badly that it's making him burst at the seams and lash out at me.

I don't know what to do.

Sincerely,

Joy

To: Joy Corvi (joy.corvi@caldwell.edu)

From: Caldwell Cupid (cupid@caldwellcupid.com)

Date: January 2, 3:10 p.m.

Subject: RE: Respect

Dear Joy,

I graduate this year, too. I know all about the confusing feelings we're holding deep in our stomachs. You're right. The future is scary.

That doesn't excuse Luca lashing out at you.

If anything, he should be understanding. He's not the only one feeling all the emotions that come with senior year winding down. He's allowed to feel the pressure, but he shouldn't take his feelings out on you.

My friends are staying in NYC for college. But I'm not. We're okay with the change because we know it's how we'll become the best versions of ourselves.

From what you've told me, I don't think Luca is okay with the change. But it's not your responsibility to ensure he is.

Sincerely,

Caldwell Cupid 💘

CHAPTER TWELVE

NATHANIEL

"So," I say when Joy comes into the study room later that day. "Do you have any ideas for topics we can propose to Mr. Baumann?"

"No." She sits down on the purple cushioned chair next to me, and we angle our chairs toward each other. "Sorry." Joy swallows the word, her mouth hanging open the slightest bit.

And even though we're sitting close enough that our knees almost touch, she's not looking at me.

She's looking through me.

"That's okay," I say, more to fill the silence than anything. "I . . . haven't, either."

Joy's shoulders collapse into themselves and for one horrified second, I think I've made her cry somehow, but instead, she's laughing.

The sound—loud and sweet, almost like a burst of

music—fills my whole chest. I've never made her laugh like this before.

"Okay." She smiles a little bit. "Maybe we should—"

"Wait, were you okay? This morning?"

"I-I . . ." Joy looks out the window, down at Forty-Second Street bustling below us. "Yeah," she settles on. "I'm okay now. Just worried about graduation, like everyone else."

"I'm not," I murmur, facing our reflections in the glass.

"Really?" Joy doesn't look directly at me, but her eyes slide over to my reflection. "Not at all?"

"Nope," I say. "I know what I want to do with the rest of my life."

"Do you, or is it just because everyone in your family is a doctor?" Joy asks. "Is continuing the tradition enough to make you happy? You're not afraid it's a mistake?"

Joy's words sink into my brain, and for a moment I think about how satisfying it would be to write more than just secret love letters for other students. But I don't dwell on it. I don't have time to. Besides, I don't really have to choose one or the other.

"I'm not scared," I say. "I want to be a doctor to help people, as cliché as that sounds."

"No, no, no." The words fly out of Joy's mouth as if she can't possibly say them fast enough. "I get it." She glances over at me, her eyes a brief flash of ocean blue. She raises her eyebrows, a quiet smirk on her face. "Maybe you'll get your wish, and we'll work in the same hospital together." I open my mouth, but then she nudges my knee with hers. A heat crawls up my leg at the touch. "That was a joke," she murmurs. "My attempt at one anyway. I'm . . . not really good at humor." She pauses.

"That makes two of us." I'm whispering now—even though there's no reason to.

"That would be kind of nice, actually. I know we aren't friends or anything like that," she continues quickly. "You have your friends and I have mine. But it would be kind of nice to keep doing better than you in all our classes."

I'm quiet long enough for the sounds of the city to fill the room. Cars. Double-decker tourist buses. Taxis. People. Sounds I've known my whole life. And all sounds I'll be leaving behind in seven months when I move to California for college.

But maybe I won't be leaving Joy behind.

"Nathaniel?" Joy prompts. "Where did you go?" She waves a hand in front of my eyes.

"Sorry." I exhale. Running my hands down my face, I peer at her once my fingers are steepled together below my chin. "That would actually be really nice."

"Yeah, right." She laughs. "I bet you can't wait to walk away from me after graduation."

"Is that what you are worried about?" I murmur. "Not me, but of Valentina, Yasmine, and Luca walking away from you after graduation?"

"No." Joy shakes her head. "But also yes."

Joy's eyes widen. An ocean so vast and so impossibly deep I would do anything to dive into it. I am so used to there being a fire in those eyes when she looks at me, but right now they are calm. It's silent between us for a moment before she straightens her back, turning to gaze out at Forty-Second Street once again. "Have you been accepted anywhere yet?"

"I'm going to the California Institute of Biology," I tell her.

"Me too." The corners of her eyes crinkle into a smile as she tells me her secret. "I accepted this morning. I guess the rivalry will continue."

"I know," I murmur, the words getting tangled in my throat. "The world has space for the two top students at this school after all." I blink at the world outside falling dark under the navy blue of oncoming night. Joy opens her mouth to speak, but then her phone chimes from the front pouch of her backpack. She looks at the screen and hurries out of her seat.

"I have to go," she says. "It's getting late, and my moms want me home."

"I'll walk to the subway with you."

"I'd like that," she says, smiling.

And the floor slips out from under me. Something inside me knows this is my moment. I should tell her the truth—that I'm Caldwell Cupid. But I'm afraid that would ruin what happened in this room today.

I'm scared things would go back to normal.

To: Caldwell Cupid (cupid@caldwellcupid.com)

From: Joy Corvi (joy.corvi@caldwell.edu)

Date: January 5, 6:13 p.m.

Subject: Foolishness & Future

Dear Cupid,

I have news! I'll be attending the California Institute of Biology. I formally accepted the admissions offer yesterday.

I'm nervous, and sad to be so far away from my family and friends. But CIB is the best of the best. I'm so excited. Because I know it's what's best for me, but also for another reason. Though the second reason is kind of foolish . . .

Sincerely,

Joy

To: Joy Corvi (joy.corvi@caldwell.edu)

From: Caldwell Cupid (cupid@caldwellcupid.com)

Date: January 5, 6:20 p.m.

Subject: RE: Foolishness & Future

Dear Joy,

We're in high school. A little foolishness is expected!

You can't leave me hanging like this!

Sincerely,

Caldwell Cupid 💘

To: Caldwell Cupid (cupid@caldwellcupid.com)
From: Joy Corvi (joy.corvi@caldwell.edu)
Date: January 5, 9:01 p.m.
Subject: RE: RE: Foolishness & Future

Dear Cupid,

CIB has a great reputation, and it's my mom's alma mater. Those are my practical reasons.

The other reason is . . . a boy.

But it's not what you think! Nathaniel is sort of my academic nemesis. He is the smartest person I know, even though I would never tell him that.

I just found out that he is also going to CIB in the fall, too. It might be silly, but I think he makes me a better student, since I always have to keep up with him.

I'm honestly awed by his mind.

I think he feels the same about me.

How are you handling the fact that you're leaving, and all your friends are staying in NYC?

Sincerely,
Joy

P.S. I'm sorry if you're not used to these conversations. You're really easy to talk to. I hope you feel the same.

To: Joy Corvi (joy.corvi@caldwell.edu)

From: Caldwell Cupid (cupid@caldwellcupid.com)

Date: January 6, 1:11 a.m.

Subject: RE: RE: RE: Foolishness & Future

Dear Joy,

I do like talking to you. It's a nice break from putting together love letters for everyone else who writes to me.

To answer your question: I know that college is a point where friend groups can change. Not fracture, but change.

I'm handling that oncoming change as best as I can, I think. I'll miss my friends. And they'll miss me. But I try to remind myself that the reason we will miss each other is because we love each other. So much.

We can prepare for the distance all we want. But missing your friends? It's something I don't think we can prepare ourselves for.

Maybe that's what Luca is focusing on.

Sincerely,

Caldwell Cupid ❤

To: Caldwell Cupid (cuipid@caldwellcupid.com)
From: Joy Corvi (joy.corvi@caldwell.edu)
Date: January 6, 1:20 a.m.
Subject: RE: RE: RE: RE: Foolishness & Future

Dear Cupid,

I think you're right.

We had a fight on New Year's Eve and haven't spoken. We've never really fought before. When we were kids, he defended me on the playground from bullies who made fun of my hand. (I have cerebral palsy, so my left wrist is perpetually bent. I don't think I mentioned that before, but I will admit it's nice to talk to someone without their eyes immediately zeroing in on my disability and not knowing what the polite thing to do is.)

Luca and I have been best friends ever since the day my family moved in across the hall from his. We're the kind of friends who take care of each other.

I'm going to miss him just as much as he'll miss me. I never thought loving someone would be painful.

I don't want him to hurt. I don't want you to hurt, either.

Sincerely,

Joy

To: Joy Corvi (joy.corvi@caldwell.edu)

From: Caldwell Cupid (cupid@caldwellcupid.com)

Date: January 6, 1:45 a.m.

Subject: RE: RE: RE: RE: RE: Foolishness & Future

Dear Joy,

I don't want you to hurt, either.

Sincerely,

Cupid

To: Caldwell Cupid (cupid@caldwellcupid.com)

From: Joy Corvi (joy.corvi@caldwell.edu)

Date: January 6, 2:00 a.m.

Subject: RE: RE: RE: RE: RE: RE: Foolishness & Future

Dear Cupid,

I'm sad, but there are going to be so many happy parts. Plus, we'll still keep them in our lives. We'll text them, call them, video chat with them, visit them during breaks . . . All of that.

Sincerely,

Joy

To: Joy Corvi (joy.corvi@caldwell.edu)

From: Caldwell Cupid (cupid@caldwellcupid.com)

Date: January 6, 2:22 a.m.

Subject: RE: RE: RE: RE: RE: RE: RE: Foolishness & Future

Dear Joy,

But what about each other? Is it okay to keep writing to you?

Sincerely,

Cupid

To: Caldwell Cupid (cupid@caldwellcupid.com)

From: Joy Corvi (joy.corvi@caldwell.edu)

Date: January 6, 2:30 a.m.

Subject: RE: RE: RE: RE: RE: RE: RE: RE: Foolishness & Future

Dear Cupid,

Absolutely. As long as you write to me, I'll write to you.

Sincerely,

Joy

CHAPTER THIRTEEN
JOY

Luca had been going out of his way to avoid me. Until after AP English today, when he walks over to me as we exit Miss Neilson's classroom.

"Hi." Luca's voice is so scratchy, it almost sounds unused. And for a second, I wonder if he's talked much at all this week. Outside of our group, Luca doesn't have any other friends.

Not that I really do, either.

"Hey." My reply is dragged down by exhaustion. When Valentina and Yasmine asked why I was so tired, I lied and said I was up late studying. Luckily, they believed me.

"I—" Luca begins. "The therapy dogs are in the library. Do you want to—"

"—pet dogs for an hour?" I finish, smiling. "Absolutely."

"Great!" Luca clumsily returns my smile, and I notice Yasmine and Valentina share a quick glance and their shoulders relax.

The four of us head toward the library, which is bustling with activity because even a week into the second semester, we're already looking for a way to relieve stress—especially the seniors.

"Hey, Yasmine!" Vikram waves from over in the corner where he and Declan are petting a golden retriever wearing a galaxy-patterned vest.

"Hi!" Yasmine smiles when we join them, all of us reaching for the puppy, who is more than happy to receive extra attention.

"This is Star Fruit," Declan introduces us, rubbing the dog between their ears. "All the therapy dogs are named after fruits."

"With appropriate vests, too," Vikram adds. "There's Strawberry, Banana, and Dragon Fruit. But Star Fruit is the best, aren't you, girl?"

As if saying yes, Star Fruit flops over onto her back so that we can all pet her belly, her tongue lolling out of her mouth.

"Hey, how are you feeling about the cheerleading competition this weekend?" Luca asks Vikram and Yasmine. His voice is still shaky, but petting Star Fruit seems to have loosened him up a bit.

"We'll do amazing," Vikram says confidently.

Yasmine nods, smiling at him. "Just like always."

"Be sure to text us when you get to Saratoga Springs, okay, babe?" Valentina cuddles into her. "I'm going to miss you."

"I will." Yasmine leans her head on Val's shoulder. "We're

only gone until Sunday. I'll text you when we get back, too."

Declan looks up from petting Star Fruit, his eyes on Vikram. "Keep me and Nathaniel posted, too!"

I reach for Star Fruit's belly. Her fur is thick and soft, almost silky, the same honey color as Nathaniel's hair. *Oh God, what am I thinking—*

"Where is Nathaniel?" I ask.

Luca's blazer rustles beside me, and try as I might to tell myself it's just because he reached for Star Fruit, I can't.

"He went home," Vikram explains. "His sister wanted company to a doctor's appointment."

"Plus, he can't be around dogs." Declan leans back on his hands. "They trigger his asthma."

"I have asthma, too," Luca points out shortly. His hands fall away from Star Fruit, and she looks positively offended at the lack of attention. "I'm fine around them."

"W-Well, asthma affects everyone differently," I tell him.

Luca shrugs, not looking at me. "I guess you're right."

Declan looks between us. The understanding in his green eyes makes my stomach sink, and for a second, I wonder exactly how much Nathaniel's friends know about me and him. If they know about the kiss on the cheek; the arguing on Christmas Day; the quiet, gentle conversation we had in the library earlier this week. "Hey," Declan says, turning to Valentina. "Um. Did you do the astronomy homework yet?"

"Yes!" Valentina replies, beaming.

"Can you explain the different between a red giant and blue dwarf star?" Declan asks. "Can there be a red dwarf and a blue giant?"

Valentina adjusts her glasses before diving into an impromptu lecture on star cycles. As she talks, pausing to give Star Fruit belly rubs, Luca relaxes against me. But—just like on Christmas Eve—he doesn't say anything.

The entire walk back to our apartment building, I keep wondering how much Declan and Vikram know about my and Nathaniel's . . . whatever it is. Friendship? Relationship?

"Hey." Luca nudges me when we reach the lobby of our apartment building. "Why are you so quiet?"

"No reason," I lie, practically tripping over the words.

"She probably has a lot on her mind," Yasmine says. "Now that she's going to CIB—"

"Wait. You are?" Luca cuts her off, his eyes growing wide as he leans against a corkboard advertising events happening in Union Square Park just across the street. "You accepted? You're officially going to *California*? You're serious?"

I nod.

"Are you . . ." Luca seems to catch himself and lowers his voice. He moves his hands around, a gesture Ma does when words won't convey everything she needs to say. "Nervous?"

"No," I splutter. "Well, yes. I'm also not nervous, but"—I

close my eyes so tightly that circles of light pop across my vision when I open them—"it's not just that. I . . ." The letter hovers on my tongue. ". . . I was really nervous, but then Caldwell Cupid said something—"

Valentina and Yasmine gasp and I realize what I just let slip.

"You've been writing to them?!" Valentina clasps her hands in front of her, her glasses teetering on the edge of her nose.

"Joy!" Yasmine bounces on the balls of her feet. "Is there someone you *like*? Who is it?"

"N-No." I shake my head, my spastic left hand waggling along with the motion. It's raised up to the same level as my breasts again. "No, it's not like that. I—I just like talking to them."

"Talking to them?" Luca repeats, adjusting his glasses. "About who?"

"Um." I gaze out the front doors, studying the entrance to Union Square Park as thoughts tumble in my head. "No one! Not about love or anything," I add, turning back to my friends. "Don't get excited. It's just . . . nice to have someone to talk to."

"Why?" Luca pushes on the bridge of his glasses. "Like you didn't have anyone to talk to before? What about us? What about me?"

"You?" I repeat, my eyes narrowing. "You haven't been speaking to me at all lately."

"Oh, c'mon." Luca sighs. "I was mad at you for a week, Joy. Get over it."

"Get over it?!" I retort. "Why were you so m-mad at me, anyway?" A thought grips me, hard enough to make my head hurt. "Was it actually about California, or was it more about Nathaniel?"

"Nate?!" Luca spits out his name. "He has nothing to do with this. I mean . . ." He closes his eyes, holding his scrunched-up forehead with his thumb and pointer finger. ". . . Joy, how could you not tell me about CIB?"

"If you hadn't been in your own feelings, you would've known about Joy's college plans," Yasmine says.

"Are you two really okay with this?" Luca asks, turning his gaze to them.

"She's going to one of the top nursing schools in the country," Val adds. "I'm not only okay with it, I am proud of her and happy for her."

Yasmine wraps an arm around me. "If you really cared about Joy," she says, "you would be, too."

"Of course I'm proud of her." Luca pushes off the wall, his voice weak. As he walks toward the elevators, I watch as the light flitters across his lenses, magnifying the tears welling up in his eyes. "I just thought I knew you better, Joy."

To: Caldwell Cupid (cupid@caldwellcupid.com)

From: Joy Corvi (joy.corvi@caldwell.edu)

Date: February 10, 11:11 p.m.

Subject: I'm Sorry

Dear Cupid,

I'm sorry I haven't written for a while. I've just been busy with school. I am supposed to be working with Nathaniel to figure out an idea for a science night at the elementary school. (We're meeting at his house on Valentine's Day, of all days.)

I've also had a lot on my mind. Beyond that.

Have you been okay these last few weeks?

Sincerely,

Joy

To: Joy Corvi (joy.corvi@caldwell.edu)

From: Caldwell Cupid (cupid@caldwellcupid.com)

Date: February 10, 11:55 p.m.

Subject: RE: I'm Sorry

Dear Joy,

You don't need to apologize to me. I know how hectic senior year is. I'm the youngest of four, so I've seen my siblings go through it, too. And now it's our turn.

To be honest, I thought you had maybe found someone after all and didn't need to write to me anymore. What's on your mind? Are you okay?

Sincerely,

Cupid

To: Joy Corvi (joy.corvi@caldwell.edu)

From: Caldwell Cupid (cupid@caldwellcupid.com)

Date: February 11, 12:07 a.m.

Subject: RE: RE: I'm Sorry

Dear Cupid,

I asked you first.

Sincerely,

Joy

To: Joy Corvi (joy.corvi@caldwell.edu)
From: Caldwell Cupid (cupid@caldwellcupid.com)
Date: February 11, 12:20 a.m.
Subject: RE: RE: RE: I'm Sorry

Dear Joy,

You did. I'm okay. I just have a lot on my mind, too. Can you tell me what's on yours?

Sincerely,

Cupid

To: Caldwell Cupid (cupid@caldwellcupid.com)

From: Joy Corvi (joy.corvi@caldwell.edu)

Date: February 11, 12:42 a.m.

Subject: RE: RE: RE: RE: I'm Sorry

Dear Cupid,

For someone who gives out love advice to other people, you're sure not adept at *answering* questions about yourself.

Sincerely,

Joy

To: Joy Corvi (joy.corvi@caldwell.edu)

From: Caldwell Cupid (cupid@caldwellcupid.com)

Date: February 11, 1:33 a.m.

Subject: RE: RE: RE: RE: RE: I'm Sorry

Dear Joy,

You're right. I suppose I'm fine asking people questions. I need all the information I can get in order to write the perfect love letter.

I'm not sure where to begin! There are a couple of things keeping me awake right now:

1) I'm pansexual. My friends know and accept me. But, most of my family has no idea. And I'm feeling some sort of obligation (?) to come out to them before I go to college. So they know me completely before I leave? Is that ridiculous?
2) The last time I told them anything about myself, my parents made such a big deal about it. When I told them I wanted to be a romance writer, they said I was foolish, that "my practical career choice would be enough." If only they knew I spent so much of my time writing love letters.
3) I've also been thinking a lot about you. But I don't really have a problem losing sleep over you.

That's enough rambling from me. Your turn, Miss Corvi.

Sincerely,

Cupid

To: Caldwell Cupid (cupid@caldwellcupid.com)

From: Joy Corvi (joy.corvi@caldwell.edu)

Date: February 11, 2:00 a.m.

Subject: RE: RE: RE: RE: RE: RE: I'm Sorry

Dear Cupid,

Please don't feel pressured to come out to your family until you're ready.

Neither of my moms had it easy coming out, though. Ma is from an Italian American family with deep Catholic roots, and Momma is from a southern Baptist family. Though they love the cultures they were raised in, we're not religious, simply because religion hasn't been the kindest to us.

When I came out as asexual, they embraced me with their whole, entire hearts. I've never known anything but love from them.

I don't want you to put yourself anywhere close to what my moms experienced in coming out. Please know that you're valid, regardless of who knows your truth.

As for your future, you can have both a practical and creative career, you know.

And as for me keeping you awake, I won't apologize. You're doing the same to me. But I don't mind at all.

Sincerely,

Joy

To: Joy Corvi (joy.corvi@caldwell.edu)

From: Caldwell Cupid (cupid@caldwellcupid.com)

Date: February 11, 2:10 a.m.

Subject: RE: RE: RE: RE: RE: RE: RE: I'm Sorry

Dear Joy,

I'm glad to know that I keep you awake and that you don't mind it. Now it's your turn. You can tell me anything.

Sincerely,

Cupid

To: Caldwell Cupid (cupid@caldwellcupid.com)

From: Joy Corvi (joy.corvi@caldwell.edu.)

Date: February 11, 2:15 a.m.

Subject: Are We Flirting?

Dear Cupid,

Are you flirting with me?

Sincerely,

Joy

To: Joy Corvi (joy.corvi@caldwell.edu)

From: Caldwell Cupid (cupid@caldwellcupid.com)

Date: February 11, 2:22 a.m.

Subject: RE: Are We Flirting?

Dear Joy,

What would you say if I was?

Sincerely,

Cupid

February 14th

Joy (11:00 a.m.): I'm on my way over now.

Nathaniel (11:02 a.m.): Good. Franny has barred me from coming downstairs until you show up. Or until she leaves for her Valentine's Day date. Whichever comes first.

CHAPTER FOURTEEN

NATHANIEL

"Nathaniel!" Franny sings, her alto voice carrying up the stairs. "Joy is here! Come downstairs!"

"Finally!" I say. Springing up from my desk chair, I bolt out of my room and down the stairs. I'm so focused on my socked feet hitting the steps that I don't look up until I've reached the entryway.

That's when I see Joy standing by the front door.

And my jaw almost becomes unhinged.

Her coat is folded across her arm, and she's wearing a long-sleeved, soft pink floral-patterned dress that falls to her knees, paired with a matching headband.

"Hi." Curse my voice for wanting to hide in my throat.

"Hi." Joy gives me a small smile, smoothing down the skirt of her dress. "I—I didn't dress up for you," she says once her eyes meet mine again.

"Of course." I wheeze. "Um. You look—"

"I dress up every Valentine's Day," Joy bursts out. "Feeling beautiful. It's a—a thing I like to do on holidays, no matter how small."

"Oh, honey, you are always beautiful," Franny says just as I was about to say the same thing. *Oh my God, I was about to say the same thing!*

"Are you leaving for your date?" I say, pulling myself together.

"Yes!" Franny claps her hands.

"Ha!" I cackle. "I was right; it is a date!"

"That was"—Franny's cheeks turn as pink as the turtleneck hugging her swollen belly—"I just—You know what, never mind. I'm going to be late if I stay here any longer trying to explain myself. Daniel made reservations; I can't be late."

"Oooh, he made reservations!" Joy teases, shimmying her shoulders. "That sounds date-like."

I gasp, leaning against the stair banister, pressing the back of my hand to my forehead and gazing up at the ceiling. "Good heavens, dear sister! Shall I inform the townspeople of your impending engagement?"

"Stuff it." Franny elbows me in the side, smirking up at me. "We're just friends, that's all."

"Daniel Ramirez is also *Warren's* best friend, isn't he?" I continue, massaging my rib cage as I take my inhaler from my jeans pocket.

"Daniel Ramirez?" Joy repeats from behind my sister. "As in Valentina's older brother? He's a doctor, too."

"Yes, he's an ob-gyn." Franny sucks in her cheeks, her eyes playful as I smirk. "What's your point?"

"Falling for your brother's best friend is the definition of a cliché, right?" I say, smirking. I take one puff of my inhaler, then another, noting that I really must learn to stop running down the stairs for purely theatrical purposes.

"Do you people even know anyone who isn't a doctor?" Joy jokes.

Franny snorts. "We try not to make a habit of it," she says, her eyes lighting up. "Here, I want you and Joy to see this. C'mon, follow me. I have to go soon." She waddles into the living room, humming.

"Well," I say as Joy and I walk the short distance into the living room. "We can't keep your boyfriend—" I choke on the end of my sentence. "Oh my God."

"Oh my God," Joy echoes.

"Francine." I whip my gaze to my sister. She's standing off to the side, next to the armchair, hugging her belly as she shakes with giggles. "What did you do?"

"I made the place festive for you two," she explains airily, waving her hand around. "I figured *studying* on *Valentine's Day* should at least be fun."

The backs of the couches and armchair are draped with heart-patterned throw blankets I'm positive I've never seen before. There is one of those life-size teddy bears wearing a pink bow patterned with red hearts sitting in the middle of the couch. The lampshades have been swapped out for magenta ones that give the light around the room a warm glow.

But the most mortifying part? Even more so than the teddy bear?

The red and pink rose petals strewn across every surface and floorboard, as if a flower shop exploded.

"Well." Franny purses her lips, supporting her back as she breezes out of the room. "Your reactions have made my day. Now I need to go meet Daniel."

Both Joy and I wait until the door clicks shut behind her before sitting down on the couch—with the massive teddy bear between us.

"Um." I drum my hands on my knees, my fingers sounding impossibly loud on the denim. "Shall we discuss ideas for the elementary school science night?" I say, attempting to distract her from the pink mess surrounding us.

"Yeah." Joy strains as she leans forward to look at me. "I-I was thinking something simple. We don't want to scare them away from science or anything."

"Exactly," I say. "Simple but engaging so that they might want to be like us someday."

Joy pauses, long enough for me to practically hear the words churning around inside her head. "Two people in a living room that looks like Cupid himself projectile vomited everywhere?"

Before I have a chance to overthink her scarily specific word choice, I sputter, "No. I meant like . . . headed to the California Institute of Biology."

Joy flops back against the couch, sending pink flower petals flying in the air. "Sorry," she says. "I can't strain my body like that for very long."

"I'm the one who's sorry," I blurt out, the heat on my cheeks trickling down my neck. "I had no idea Franny was doing all"—I pick up a handful of the petals, tossing them around—"this."

"It's okay. It's kind of . . . sweet?" she says, shrugging.

"Sweet?" I repeat, raising my eyebrows. "Really? It seems kind of . . ."

"Excessive, yeah." Joy pauses. "But—But it's pretty funny. And you can tell she had fun doing this."

The teddy bear is now between us, and since I can't see her eyes, I suddenly feel brave. "I have fun doing this," I say quickly.

"Doing what?" Joy asks.

"Studying," I say.

"Of course you like it," she replies.

"No," I practically splutter. "But I mean I like studying. With you."

She's so quiet that I'm almost tempted to stand up from the couch so I can actually read her expression instead of just imagining the worst possible thing. Is she uncomfortable? Why did I say that? What are we supposed to do now? Do I apologize—

"Oh." The word is so gentle that it's barely more than a puff of air. "Nathaniel, I—I like studying with you, too. It's nice."

It's nice. It's nice. It's nice.

My heart beats in time with her compliment.

"Let's get started." Joy gets to her feet, digging her right hand into her hip. Her left hand is clenched across her stomach as she walks over to me. "Here, help me up," she says, putting one foot on the coffee table and reaching out to me.

"Onto the coffee table?" I ask confusedly, raising my eyebrows. "Why?"

"Because we can't see each other with that bear between us," she points out. "And I'm too short for you to take me seriously just standing in front of you like this."

"But I do take you seriously," I reassure her. Joy's eyes snap to me, her glasses teetering on the edge of her nose. "Why else do you think I proposed the bet?"

"Nathaniel." Joy's lips quirk. "Are you indirectly paying me a compliment?"

"It's these rose petals," I mutter, knowing that I've flushed the exact same shade. "And that bear. They're all making me *feel things*."

Them and our late-night emails.

"Well." Joy's tongue flicks out of the corner of her mouth. "I still want to be on the coffee table for dramatic effect as we figure this out. Are you going to help me up?"

I grab her hips, lifting her up the short distance to the

wooden surface. My fingers dig in to where the top of her dress and its skirt meet, and for a moment, I imagine what I would say if I could tell her the truth.

Joy, I would say, *I'm Caldwell Cupid. You make me feel safe with you, and yes, I am flirting with you. I've been flirting with you for four years. And it's not to throw you off like you think.*

But it's not that easy.

So, I let go of her hips, watching as she teeters before establishing her balance. I reach out just in case she falls.

"I'm okay." She clears her throat as she bends down to retrieve a handful of the petals. "So, we need something simple, but still engaging for elementary school students," she begins.

"Right." I nod. "What's your brilliant plan?"

"Well, these float." She throws the petals she'd gathered up into the air, watching as a curtain of red and pink falls between us. "We could do an experiment with flight."

"Yes!" I bounce on the balls of my feet. "When you were a kid, did you ever like to play with maple seeds as they fell from the trees?"

"Because they look like helicopters?" Joy bends forward, almost pitching herself off the coffee table. "I've got it. I've got it. I'm fine," she says, reassuring me more than her. "Yes! I used to spin them around between my fingers—I got it!"

We clap our hands at the same time, the sharp sound echoing between us. "We'll make paper helicopters!"

"Shit!" Joy hisses.

I lunge forward as she tilts off the table. Catching her against my chest, she stands on her tiptoes, her arms wrapped around my neck, her cheek pressed to my pink sweater, right where my heart is.

"Oh God." She sucks in a shaky breath, and I listen to her own heart pump against mine. "I-I'm sorry. I'm so clumsy."

"Don't apologize," I murmur, my hand moving in soothing circles on her back. "I'm just glad I was able to catch you."

"This is so embarrassing," Joy whispers. "I know what my cerebral palsy does. Why did I think I should get up there?" She swallows, her body rigid in my arms.

"Do you. Um." Now it's my turn to swallow, and I will my voice to have an ounce of seriousness. "Do you need any help? Are you in pain anywhere? I'm sorry I'm asking so many questions."

"You only asked two," Joy murmurs, shaking her head. "No. I'm fine. Just . . . muscle spasms. Just give me a minute, please? I just need a minute."

"Yes." I breathe a sigh of relief; it's one she echoes. "Take as long as you need."

And we stand there in the middle of my living room, our arms wrapped around each other, taking in the sounds of each other's heartbeats.

But I still feel so far away from her.

To: Caldwell Cupid (cupid@caldwellcupid.com)

From: Joy Corvi (joy.corvi@caldwell.edu)

Date: February 14, 10:10 p.m.

Subject: RE: RE: Are We Flirting?

Dear Cupid,

Do you remember that boy I told you about, Nathaniel?

Sincerely,

Joy

To: Joy Corvi (joy.corvi@caldwell.edu)

From: Caldwell Cupid (cupid@caldwellcupid.com)

Date: February 14, 10:12 p.m.

Subject: RE: RE: RE: Are We Flirting?

Dear Joy,

Your rival, Nathaniel? Yes, I remember him. Has my rivals-to-lovers trope suggestion worked?

Sincerely,

Cupid

To: Caldwell Cupid (cupid@caldwellcupid.com)

From: Joy Corvi (joy.corvi@caldwell.edu)

Date: February 14, 11:11 p.m.

Subject: Falling

Dear Cupid,

Sorry to disappoint you. But, no.

At least, not yet?

Maybe we are moving toward that.

Somehow.

I'm surprised by how it makes me feel—because we've never seen eye to eye on anything. We have argued throughout our entire time as president and vice president of the Science Society. We always have to one-up each other.

Today, I fell into his arms while we were working on a science project together and I saw exactly how strong and caring he is. How he held me as my muscles spasmed and our hearts raced gave me a certain warmth. I don't think I have ever felt that way before.

In that moment, I didn't feel as though I had to prove myself. To anyone. All I had to do was be held. And I was really glad Nathaniel was there to hold me.

Sincerely,

Joy

CHAPTER FIFTEEN

NATHANIEL

It's been a little over three weeks since Joy sent me that email—and I haven't responded.

I don't know what to say.

I made Joy feel warmth when I caught her, held her so she didn't fall, as our hearts raced together. I made her feel as though she didn't need to prove herself. For once.

I'm sitting with a blanket on my lap as possible replies tumble around in my head.

A frigid February has flowed into a chilly March. I'm still wired from seeing Vikram take the stage as Pippin earlier tonight, so it doesn't surprise me at all that it's 12:41 a.m.

"C'mon," I whisper into my palm as I press my hand to my lips. "Think of some—"

That's when I hear Franny scream downstairs.

Throwing my blanket off and grabbing my inhaler from

next to my mouse pad, I bolt out of the room, praying for my asthma to knock it off as I barrel down the stairs. I very nearly lose my footing but manage to clutch onto the banister to steady myself.

"Franny!" Her name breaks apart in my mouth. "Where are you?"

"Kitchen," she whimpers.

Running through the dining room and into the kitchen, I see her, leaning against the island in her nightgown.

Her hands are pressed to her stomach, a small puddle of water at her feet.

We're the only ones home; our parents are working the overnight shift.

"What's—What's going on?" A river of icy sweat springs to life on my back.

Franny closes her eyes, bracing her back against the island again. "My water broke."

I stare at her, barely able to croak out the next few words. "But . . ." My lungs are on fire in my chest, angry at me for running. And even though my inhaler is in my hand, I can barely move, much less put the thing between my lips. "You're only . . ."

"Thirty-three weeks," Franny finishes. "I know. It's too early. I can't believe I . . . God, I'm not—I'm not ready." Her chin quivers. "I don't know what to do."

"Franny." I walk over to her, putting my hands on her

shoulders, wondering how I'm not even shaking. "I need you to breathe." I slowly take a lungful of air, wincing as it burns all the way in, then out. "Can you do that?"

"Yeah." Her voice is quiet as she copies my breathing. "I can—" She grits her teeth, trying to blow air out from her lips as she leans against the island again. *"My back,"* she hisses.

"Another contraction?" I ask, my voice level. She nods, her eyes filling with tears, and I do the math in my head. "They're three minutes apart. Let's get you to the hospital, okay?"

March 12th

Joy (12:00 p.m.): Hey, I'm getting some supplies for our big science night. Do you think I should get different color paper? Or one uniform color?

Nathaniel (12:00 p.m.): Can you meet me at NewYork-Presbyterian, please?

Joy (12:01 p.m.): What happened? Are you hurt?

Nathaniel (12:05 p.m.): No, I helped deliver my niece. I just need someone here.

Joy (12:06 p.m.): I'll be right there.

Nathaniel (12:06 p.m.): I'm sitting outside the NICU. Just tell them you're here for Francine and they'll let you back.

CHAPTER SIXTEEN

JOY

"Hi," I say, walking up to the desk in the labor and delivery unit of NewYork-Presbyterian. "My name is Joy. I'm here to see Dr. Francine Wright?"

Brittany, one of my mom's coworkers, smiles at me. "Hi, sweetheart. This way." She leads me into a hallway lined with a long glass room. I hear Nathaniel before I see him.

"Joy!"

Brittany steps to the side, and I run to meet Nathaniel in the middle of the hallway. I throw my arms around him, and his arms curl around my back.

"I-I'm so proud of you," I gasp against his soft cotton T-shirt.

"Thank you," Nathaniel whispers, tightening his arms around me. "I—I can't believe my sister gave birth. I can't believe I *helped* her. If she . . ."

"Here." I pull away from his shirt; he loosens his arms until his fingers are holding the hem of my light blue sweater. "Let's sit down."

We take the chairs closest to us, and Nathaniel turns to me. He has deep purple bags under his eyes; his blond hair is rumpled. I've never seen him look anything less than picture perfect. Even his voice is heavy with tiredness.

"How's your niece?"

"She has neonatal respiratory distress syndrome," he says wearily, dragging his hand down his face.

"My ma's told me before about babies that have that," I say. "Is she . . . ?"

"They have her on a nasal CPAP." Nathaniel yawns, pointing to the NICU window in front of us. "You can see her if you look. She's the third one in the front."

Leaning forward, I count the incubators until I get to the third one. "Natalie," I murmur.

"Natalie Hope Wright," Nathaniel says, a small smile unfurling across his face. "Franny insisted on naming her after me. She says without me, things could've been a lot different."

"They would've," I say. "How . . . are you?"

"Me?" Nathaniel blinks. "I'm fine. Today was . . . Joy, I think today might have changed my whole life."

"What do you mean?" I ask.

"I want to be an ob-gyn," Nathaniel says quietly. "I want to help people deliver their babies, as well as provide sexual and reproductive healthcare. I want my patients to know that they are safe with me." He drags his hand down his face again, holding his chin between his thumb and pointer finger. "Just as I made sure my sister knew I was there for her." He blinks, his eyes wet. "Is that a ridiculous dream?"

I open my mouth, but before I can answer, my mom walks into the NICU. She heads straight for Natalie's incubator. Her mouth moves as she checks something, smiling gently at the tiny baby inside.

"No," I murmur. "Nathaniel. It's not ridiculous at all."

"Thank you," he whispers after a moment. "Um. Joy? I've been awake since seven a.m. yesterday." He yawns with a deep sigh. "Can I sleep on your shoulder, please?"

"Sure," I say, my voice soft.

Nathaniel melts into me, resting his head against my shoulder. I lurch a little bit—but force my shoulder back to make us both more comfortable. Warmth surges through my whole body as my heart pounds.

In minutes, I can tell he is asleep, and I listen as his chest rises and falls.

It was my turn to catch him.

CHAPTER SEVENTEEN

NATHANIEL

Natalie will be in the hospital for the next month.

Franny rarely leaves her side, and when she does, Daniel accompanies her home. Franny tells me that he kisses her each time they reach the front door. She's whispering to me about how sweet he is when Mother and Father come into the living room. As usual, they haven't been around much, so there's a lot going on around here they don't know about. "Hi," I begin a little awkwardly as they curl up on the couch together, books in hand.

Father and Mother give me matching gentle smiles.

"Can I talk to you?" I ask, readjusting myself in the armchair.

"I'll excuse myself," Franny says, flitting out of the room.

"Of course." Mother nods.

I fold my hands together and lean forward so that my elbows balance on my knees.

A few seconds of silence pass between us.

We're not the best family when it comes to verbal communication. I come by it honestly, at least.

"I have something to tell you," I say finally. After exhaling a slow, deep breath, I continue: "I know what specialty I want to go into."

"You do?" Mother beams. She puts her hand over her mouth, her rings gleaming in the lights from our lamps and ceiling fan. "Oh, Nathaniel! That's wonderful!"

"It's a special day when a Wright realizes their future in medicine," Father adds, grinning. I flush at their praise. "Well done. What have you decided?"

"Obstetrics and gynecology."

They both drop their books.

The sound of them hitting the hardwood floor is sharp in my ears. But not nearly as sharp as the silence that follows. This silence is weighted; it's pressing on my ears, seeping into my nose and down my throat until it reaches my rib cage.

It squeezes both my heart and lungs inside.

Please. Say something.

"Nathaniel." Father clears his throat, readjusting himself on the couch. "Don't be ridiculous. You're far too smart for that."

"Why is it ridiculous?" I ask, willing my voice not to fade. "It's a valid area of medicine."

"Your father is right," Mother adds gently. "You could become a neurosurgeon like him or a cardiothoracic surgeon like me or—"

"A plastic surgeon like Warren?" I finish. "Or a pediatric surgeon like Everett?"

My insides curdle when they nod.

"You don't need to waste your time being an ob-gyn," Mother chimes in.

"Waste my time?" I repeat, glaring at her. "Mother, did you forget what happened on Friday?" She looks away from me, her glassy gaze now focused on the windows. "I suppose that's possible because you weren't here. Neither of you are ever—"

"Don't you dare finish that sentence," Father cuts in, getting to his feet. His glare matches mine. "And don't you dare use that tone with your mother. Apologize to her immediately."

"You want me to apologize to her?" I rise to my feet next, hit with the startling realization that I'm taller than my father now. "I don't have anything to be sorry for."

Father spits out a humorless laugh.

"You weren't here to help Franny breathe through her contractions. To keep track of how far apart they were. To call 911 so that Franny could get to the hospital safely. To stay with her so she would have family in the delivery room. To hug her as she cried, watching her baby be taken to the NICU. You weren't there for any of it. I was."

"You're standing there," Mother finally whispers, her gaze on me again, "all proud of yourself. But why didn't you call us until after Natalie was born?"

My mouth falls open. "Because I was busy making sure my sister was safe. She deserved all my attention."

"And I didn't deserve to know she was in labor?" Mother counters.

"Are you serious right now?!" I shout.

"Nathaniel." Father's voice is full of the storm that's choking the Manhattan sky above us. "You can't expect to be a successful medical professional if you behave like this."

"Excuse me?" I drop my hands. "I won't be successful if I put the needs of my patient above all others? Do you have any idea what you're saying?"

"Enough!" Father says.

I flinch. He's never one to raise his voice. But then again, I've never challenged them this way.

"Nathaniel." Father clears his throat again, his voice only slightly below yelling. "We'll discuss this later, when you've calmed down."

"I won't change my mind," I say, walking across the living room until I'm in the hallway. "No matter how much you want me to. I get to do what I want."

I wait by the stairs, straining my ears to hear even the

slightest bit of a reply from my parents. But they say nothing. In fact, the only noise either of them makes is their bodies shifting as they pick up their books.

My head swivels from our staircase to the front door, and I walk out into the rain.

CHAPTER EIGHTEEN

NATHANIEL

I find myself at Dog and Moon, the Irish pub Declan's family owns. Declan is working, and I need to be near a friend.

When I walk inside the darkened restaurant, my shoes squelching from the rain, Declan's older sibling Cillian waves me to the bar.

"Nathaniel!" they call over the music. Flutes, fiddles, and uilleann pipes sound as familiar to me as my grandparents' Irish accents. "You'll catch your death, get over here."

"Alcohol doesn't actually get you warm," I say as I take a seat on a barstool in front of them. "It makes you colder."

Cillian raises a single, bushy red eyebrow. "Mr. Know-It-All, I'm not serving alcohol to a minor. That'd be a quick way for me to lose my job." They flex their right hand, which is the one affected by cerebral palsy. "It's already hell for disabled people to find work, so that's not happening. I can offer you this, though." They toss me a towel, the soft fibers smacking me in the face. "Dry off, Fancy Pants."

"Fancy Pants?" I repeat, spitting out the fibers that have gotten into my mouth.

"That would be a great drag name," Cillian says thoughtfully, ignoring my question. "Anyway, what brings you here? I'm expecting your brothers soon, actually!" I run the towel over my face and through my hair. "If you're looking for Declan, he's in the kitchen now and too busy to talk."

"No," I say quickly, trying to use the towel to help wring out my sweater. "I just . . . I needed somewhere to go?"

"Fair enough." Cillian studies me with green eyes that are exactly like Declan's. "I'll grab you something from the kitchen." They walk away from me and toward the serving hatch. "Declan!" Their voice fades in the cacophony of the pub. "What do we have back here to eat? Nathaniel is here and he's starved."

While I wait for Cillian, my foot jiggles against the front of the bar. Excess water drips from my sweater sleeves, and I try to squeeze it out with the towel. Anything to keep my mind from going back to my family's brownstone.

"Here you go." Cillian drops a glass of water, a corned beef sandwich, a pickle, and fries in front of me. It all smells so warm, salty, and tangy that my stomach gurgles immediately. I barely even say thank you before crunching into the sandwich. The corned beef practically melts in my mouth and chasing it with a bite of pickle is nothing short of absolutely glorious.

"Good, right?" Cillian grins at me and I nod, making their smile broaden. "Declan will be glad to know that. Even the pickles are his recipe now."

"Nathaniel." Everett's voice comes through the front door. "What are you doing here?"

"I . . ." *Am escaping from our parents because they don't support my future?* How am I supposed to finish that sentence?

"He needed food," Cillian lies smoothly. They reach across the bar, bringing Everett to their shoulder for a quick, tight hug before giving one to Warren.

"So do we." Everett smiles as both of my brothers sit on the stools next to me.

Everett's foot jiggles against the front of the bar, same as mine just was. "Is . . . Arthur here yet?"

"Yeah." Cillian hands them each a glass of cider without having to ask. "He's in the back where the stage is. Andrew just got back from a ren faire so they're catching up."

"Arthur?" I take a sip of my water, sucking in an ice cube. Warren, Everett, and Cillian have been friends for years, but I've never once heard of anyone named Arthur.

Everett's eyes flit down to his shoes, then to me, then to Warren, then to Cillian. He turns his gaze toward me again.

"Is he your colleague?" I ask.

"No." The word melts into a gentle sigh. The ease of it is reflected in his blue eyes. "Nathaniel, Arthur is my boyfriend, actually."

My stomach sails down to my ankles. "You have a boyfriend?" All these years—this whole time—I thought that I was the only queer person in my family. The news that I'm not feels like the sun washing over my skin. A warm, bright, pulsing relief.

"I do." Everett takes a sip of his drink, smiling around the rim of the glass. "We live together, too."

"Cillian, can we have our usual, please?" Warren asks.

"Sure thing." Cillian braces Everett's shoulder before walking back to the serving hatch.

"So." Everett turns fully toward me, resting his elbows on his knees. "You . . . probably have a lot of questions."

"No!" I blurt out, my insides clenching as my brother pulls a face. "I mean . . ." I polish off my pickle. "I just never expected . . ."

"Me to be gay?" Everett finishes off his cider, setting the empty glass on the bar with a clunk. "Well, when a family practically oozes heterosexuality, there's bound to be at least one outlier."

"Two." That simple number ties my vocal cords into a knot, one that pulses in my throat like a second heart.

"Two?" my brothers repeat gently. Everett leans forward, his fingers steepled beneath his chin.

"Nathaniel, you can tell us anything," Warren says. "We want you to know that, okay?"

I nod, tears pricking at the corners of my eyes. "I'm pansexual," I say, my voice fading. "I-I'm sorry I didn't tell you before." I blink, the tears now rolling down my cheeks. "Franny knows." Panic sets in. "Does that mean I need to tell Mother and Father now? I'm not ready—"

Everett cuts me off when he stands up from his barstool, sweeping me into the kind of hug that could crush ribs to powder. Warren wraps his arms around both of us from behind, and I'm suddenly squished between my brothers.

"You don't have to tell them a thing," Everett says soothingly. "Not if you don't want to. I've known I was gay for decades, and I also know how they are. But you have me, Franny, and Warren. And we love you."

"We do," Warren says.

"I love you, too," I murmur against his shoulder.

As my brothers dig into shepherd's pie and I finish off my fries, my shoulders loosen. I feel . . . lighter. Which is nice.

"So." I take a sip of my water. "How'd you meet Arthur?"

"Oh." Everett smiles around a forkful of food, mashed potatoes clinging to his bottom lip. "Here we go with the questions. Well, Arthur is a retired army medic," he explains, wiping his lips. "We met through my friend who works with the Wounded Warrior Project. He's a counselor for queer youth now," my brother continues softly. "We kept making excuses to see each other, until I finally had the courage to kiss him." He laughs a little.

"Talkin' about me when I'm not around, baby?" a voice with a Southern twang asks cheerfully. "That's rude, you know."

Everett's whole body lights up at the sound of the voice, as if the storm outside started so that my brother could borrow the sun and no one would notice.

I've seen that look before, on students who write to me. On the people to whom they hand my letters. But I've just never seen that look on my brother's face until right now.

Everett slips off the barstool to hug a handsome guy with a head of tawny brown hair and bright hazel eyes. He's sitting in a wheelchair, and his dog tags are as shiny as the chair's silver accents.

"Well, I'm sorry." Everett laughs as Arthur playfully pulls him into his lap.

"You're lucky you're cute." Arthur heaves a sigh, his massive shoulders rolling beneath a tight red T-shirt. "It's the only reason I forgive you." He plants a kiss on my brother's jaw, flexing his arms around his waist.

Everett smiles at him, his eyes crinkling. "I have someone for you to meet." He gestures to me. "This is my younger brother, Nathaniel."

Arthur offers me his hand and I shake it. His grip is strong and warm. "Arthur Oakley," he introduces himself, grinning broadly. "It's great to meet you, Nathaniel."

"Likewise." Arthur has the kind of smile that's just infectious, so I grin back at him. "Thank you for your service," I add.

"Thank you," Arthur says warmly. "It was an honor."

"How long have you been together?" My brain whirls as I realize that I am not the only person in this family who has led a life entirely separate from the one they present.

"Five years," Everett says as Arthur accepts a beer from Cillian with a smile.

"Last month. I love your brother, very much." He gives Everett a quick kiss, and my brother relaxes against him.

"I can tell he loves you, too," I say, smiling. "Are you—"

Everett's phone chimes in his hand. His face falls when he looks up at me. "It's Father."

"He texted me, too," Warren says. "He's asking if we know where you are. You didn't tell them you were coming here?"

"No." I drink the last of my water. "I . . ." I hesitate for a moment. But I guess after coming out to them, I really can tell my brothers anything. "Helping Franny deliver Natalie made me realize that I want to be an ob-gyn. And. Um. Mother and Father don't like that."

"Ah, the Wright disapproval," my brothers say in unison.

"Your choice of specialty is yours," Warren tells me. "Not theirs. You kept Franny breathing and timed her contractions.

We were super impressed when she told us the story."

"Wow." A smile flickers across my face. "Thank you."

"Tell them that your siblings support you," Warren says. "I mean, they might not agree. But you still have to do what's best for you."

I nod. "I know what I'm meant to do." Taking a deep breath, I add, "And I know that I need to convince them of that."

"Don't let their views of medicine stop you, though," Everett advises gently. "They hated when I went into pediatric surgery. But I love my work."

"And we know you will, too," Warren adds, patting my back. "Go home, and good luck."

When the door to our brownstone closes behind me, the click of the lock echoes in the entryway. A shiver travels from my shoulders and down along my arms. Spring may be around the corner, but winter is still thick in the air outside, especially at night.

For a moment, as I put my sneakers in the closet, I think I'm the only one down here.

"Nathaniel?" Mother calls from the living room. "Come in here, please."

I follow her voice. Both of my parents are still on the couch, with the throw blanket arranged over their laps and their books in their hands.

“We’ve been discussing your little outburst,” Father says. “And we’ve come to a decision.”

“We are so proud that you got into CIB,” Mother continues. “However”—she holds up her finger—“if you’re still choosing to pursue obstetrics and gynecology, we will not be paying your tuition, or your room and board.”

“I—” My mouth falls open, and a new chill races down my arms. My body aches as I wrench it away from the living room, at a loss for any words to say. I force my feet to move up each step of the staircase.

Once I reach my bedroom, I throw myself onto my bed and wriggle underneath the covers. Still in my damp sweater. Still in my jeans. Still in my socks that are plastered to my skin. My ears are ringing as my thoughts spiral.

This is it. I can’t afford to go to CIB without my parents’ help. I can’t have what I want if it doesn’t fit their idea of who I am.

To: Caldwell Cupid (cupid@caldwellcupid.com)

From: Joy Corvi (joy.corvi@caldwell.edu)

Date: March 13, 9:27 p.m.

Subject: Hello

Dear Cupid,

It's been awhile. How are you?

Sincerely,

Joy

To: Joy Corvi (joy.corvi@caldwell.edu)
From: Caldwell Cupid (cupid@caldwellcupid.com)
Date: March 13, 9:45 p.m.
Subject: RE: Hello

Dear Joy,

I think there is something you should know about Nathaniel.

He isn't who you think he is.

Maybe these letters have filled your head with false ideas of love and romance. Maybe we shouldn't write to each other anymore.

Sincerely,
Cupid

CHAPTER NINETEEN
JOY

"Nathaniel didn't speak once in class." I look toward the door. He exited as soon as the bell rang, like he couldn't leave the room quickly enough. "Or come up to my locker this morning. Do you think he's okay?"

"Don't worry about Nate," Luca says. "You have so much going on the next couple of weeks. Can I help you sort out your helicopter idea?"

Luca's been trying to be a better friend. By which I mean, not be a complete asshole.

"But we came up with the paper helicopter idea together." I leave out how that had happened on Valentine's Day. How the living room had been covered in rose petals, and how I fell into his arms.

I'm tempted to text him, but my thumb navigates to the Caldwell Academy email app instead, like my brain is telling me to just stop focusing on Nathaniel for a second. Opening the app, I click on Cupid's email and begin to read.

I think there is something you should know about Nathaniel.
He isn't who you think he is.
Maybe these letters have filled your head with false ideas of love and romance. Maybe we shouldn't write to each other anymore.

My heart drops into my stomach.

No.

No.

No.

"Oh God." The words emerge from my lips like the most fervent prayer, despite the fact that I've never once stepped foot into a church.

"Joy, don't cry." The fingers on my left hand dig into my palm. "Please."

But tears slip down my cheeks as my knuckles tighten.

"Joy." Valentina nudges me, concern wrapped around her voice. "Is something wrong?"

"N-No," I lie. "J-Just a muscle spasm."

We leave Mr. Baumann's classroom, and as my friends head upstairs for the next class period, I spot Nathaniel down the hall.

"Nathaniel!"

Try as I might to convince myself otherwise, my palsied legs are simply not meant for speed walking. It's hard to catch up to someone who's a full fourteen inches taller than me.

He stops so fast that I nearly bang into his back. When he turns around, I can see that his eyes are glassy and that his face is blotchy. "Yes, Joy?" he asks scratchily. "What is it?"

"I—I. Um." I pause, unsure of how to proceed. "I just wanted to make sure you were okay. You've been kind of quiet."

"Oh." Nathaniel steps backward, almost gulping down the word. "Thank you. But I'm fine. I'll see you later."

He turns on his heel and walks away, leaving me in the hallway with other students streaming past. Conversations press against my ears. College acceptances. Prom. Graduation. Every topic imaginable, except the short one swirling between my ears.

Once the last class of the day ends, I head to the science wing's lecture hall for our Caldwell Science Society meeting.

"All right!" Mr. Baumann sings from his spot before the whiteboard. "We're missing Nathaniel, so let's just give him a few minutes, then we can dive into our plans for the elementary school science night next week."

Nathaniel and I haven't spoken since the hallway this morning, so I have no idea what's going to happen when he arrives. He's not one to act without a plan, and he's definitely not usually late. I check the time. It's 3:05 p.m.

The door to the lecture hall opens, and I drop my phone. I'm grateful that it tumbles to the speckled linoleum floor because it gives me a chance to hide my face until I can control my emotions.

"I'm here." Nathaniel coughs. "Sorry I'm late."

At his words, my abdomen cramps up. I hug my torso, willing it to stop. The last thing I need right now is my period.

"No worries!" Mr. Baumann says cheerfully. "You're here now and that's what matters. Now, the elementary school science night is after spring break next week, so we only have a little while to finalize our plans." He spreads his hands, stepping aside. "Joy, Nathaniel, the floor is yours."

We walked to the center of the room. But before either of us actually says anything, Nathaniel erupts into a coughing fit. He turns away, hacking into his elbow.

"Nathaniel?" Mr. Baumann asks, concern in his voice. "Are you all right?"

Nathaniel faces our teacher. The color is high in his cheeks, his eyes shimmery. He turns away to cough again, his shoulders quaking with each forceful motion. "Sorry," he wheezes.

"Don't apologize," our teacher reassures him.

"Are you sick?" Yasmine asks.

"No." Nathaniel shakes his head, running his hand through his rumpled hair. "It's just my asthma acting up."

But his eyes are tired, and his forehead is shining with sweat. "Can I . . . see something?" I ask, tentative.

He shrugs and I lean forward, brushing his hair back as I press my hand to his forehead. A jolt passes along my right arm at my skin touching his. It's quick, replaced by an uncomfortable warmth radiating at the center of my palm.

"Nathaniel," I murmur. "You—You're burning up." His eyes flash at my words and my hand falls away. "You should go home."

"Why?" he finishes, venom having been injected into his voice. "So you can do this all on your own and steal the credit?"

"Of course not," I stammer.

"You know what," Nathaniel retorts. "This is all getting too weird, Joy. You're way too attached to me."

My mouth falls open.

"Here we go again," Luca whispers.

"You're the one who texted me to come to the hospital to be there for you," I continue. "And then *you* fell asleep on *my* shoulder."

"He what?" Valentina whispers. "Babe, did you know about this?"

"No," Yasmine whispers back. "He hasn't told me anything."

"Interesting," Declan murmurs.

"You didn't have to come!" Nathaniel shouts. "I—I would've been fine!"

I get to my feet, swinging my backpack across my shoulders. "I'm sorry, Mr. Baumann. I can email you the plan I have written up for the helicopters."

I turn on my heel so sharply that I almost lose my balance but manage to get out of the lecture hall, slamming the door behind me. Nathaniel follows me out, so I speed up as much as I can. Halfway down the hall, he catches up to me.

"What?" I hiss. "For someone who basically just called me clingy, *you* sure seem to be unable to leave *me* alone."

"Nate, I think you should just go." Luca is suddenly standing in between us.

"Let them talk." Valentina follows, pulling Luca out of the way.

"I'm not going to let him be rude to Joy for no reason," Luca tells her. "He's always been a jerk to her."

"My name is Nathaniel." He steps aside, raising his gaze from his loafers to look at Luca. "Not Nate. Or Nathan. I don't like nicknames."

"Well," Luca says, reaching my side. "I don't like you." He slides his arm through mine. "C'mon." Together, my friends and I walk down the hall and out of the building. The start of Declan, Vikram, and Nathaniel's conversation fades into murmured whispers.

When we reach the cacophony of Manhattan outside, the noise presses on my ears. Uncomfortably so, as if every sound, no matter how small, has suddenly become impossibly loud.

I slide out of Luca's arm to place both of my hands over my ears, even as my left one scrabbles at the side of my face.

"You're okay," Luca tells me, his voice muffled. "I'm here. You're okay. Let's head home."

CHAPTER TWENTY

JOY

Emotions bubble in my chest the entire ride home on the Q train. They press against my ribs, squeezing my lungs and heart.

I wipe at the tears that have managed to slide down my cheeks when I walk into the lobby and into the elevator. When Luca and I reach our floor, we hug Yasmine and Valentina goodbye.

"You should come in," he says gently. "I don't want you to be alone right now." And it's so kind that I follow him into his apartment, gratefully.

Maybe Luca was right about Nathaniel. Maybe Cupid is, too. Maybe I should stop ignoring all the signs in front of me and stop caring about him.

Because I do.

I care about Nathaniel.

Shaking that thought of out my head, I try to smile as Luca's sister, Lena, waves at me from the kitchen. She's wearing a bright yellow robotics T-shirt and a pair of paint-spattered jeans and eating pink-frosted animal crackers.

"Hi, Joy!" She grins, her eyes shift to Luca, and she can tell something is up. "I'm just going to go do homework in my room. Promise not to eavesdrop." She giggles, scampering away.

Luca waits to hear the click of her bedroom door before turning to me. "C'mon." He leads me to the brown couch in the living room. When we sit down, he nudges my knee with his. "Do you want to talk about it, now that we are alone?"

I sigh. Leaning back against the plush cushions, I stare up at the ceiling fan. "I'm not sure what to say. I'm not sure what I'm feeling," I mumble. "Is that pathetic?"

"No." Luca slings his arm around my shoulders. "You're confused. So." He taps on the edge of my blazer, and I look in his direction. "What's on your mind?"

I raise my eyebrows as more cramps twist my stomach. "Is this your way of apologizing?"

Luca nods. "I . . . know I haven't been the best friend lately. And I'm sorry about that. I really am. I'm just going to miss you when you go to CIB, you know?"

"I know," I murmur. "I-I'll miss you, too."

Luca straightens his back. "Was all that back there because you're going to miss Nate, too?" he asks. "Are you . . ." His eyes flit away for a second, toward the ceiling fan, before returning to me. "Do you have feelings for him?"

"I . . ." The truth burns in my chest. "I thought I did," I whisper. "But now I think I might have read the whole situation wrong."

"Joy." Luca angles his whole body toward mine, my name nothing more than a whisper of breath in his mouth. His arm drops from my shoulders, his hand thwacking on the knees of his plum-colored school pants. "I've been waiting for the right time to tell you this, but it seems like maybe there is no perfect time. The reason I got so upset that you're leaving is because I love you."

"Of course you do," I say soothingly. "I love you, too."

"No," Luca interjects, hushed. "Joy, it's more than that." He shuts his eyes. Light flashes across his glasses' lenses before he opens them again. "I *like* you. Okay? I always have."

I stare at him as the truth sinks in. My stomach twists.

My friends were right.

"That's why I don't want you to leave me," Luca continues quickly, as if he can't possibly say the words fast enough—or with enough reverence. "Please—"

Luca cuts himself off and leans forward suddenly, grabbing me by the shoulders and crashing his lips into mine. His eyes are closed, but mine are open, focused on the windows over his shoulder as his saliva drips down my chin.

Holy shit.

Luca is kissing me—

I pull away from him, the force sending me tumbling onto the carpet. The fall makes pain zip up my arms. "I'm sorry," I say without meeting his eyes as I get to my feet. "I need to go."

"Joy." I barely hear my name, but I turn around. The color has drained from Luca's face. "Wait," he says. "Please."

"No," I squeak. "No, I don't think I will. Let's just pretend this never happened, okay?" My left hand bunches into a fist. "C-Can we do that, please?"

"Sure." Luca squawks the word more than says it, but before I can think too much about that, I'm out of his unit and in mine, slamming the door behind me.

"Whoa." Momma meets me in the hallway, Ma not far behind. "Where's the fire, baby?"

"Nowhere!" I yell, running past them. "I—I just need . . ."

"Joy." Ma gently takes my arm, turning me around to face her. Her brow knits, like I'm one of the babies she takes care of. "Sweetheart, did something happen?"

"No," I mumble, realizing that my fresh batch of tears gives it away. "I've just had a bit of a day. And I'm having period cramps, on top of everything. And . . ." I worry the edge of my blazer with my right hand while my left is fisted up near my breasts. "Um." I look at the hardwood floor as Pomegranate weaves through my legs. "Luca kissed me."

"He kissed you?!" Their gasps turn my face the approximate shade of my hair.

"But—But I didn't want him to kiss me!" I wail, walking backward down the hall until I reach the bathroom. "It was disgusting! He got his saliva all over my chin."

"Oh." My moms blink at me, then at each other.

"I—I don't even like Luca like that!" I pause, leaning against the door.

"You don't?" Ma asks, genuinely confused. I raise my eyebrows at her. "Sorry, you two are just so close, we always sort of assumed. Not hoped or anything! But assumed."

"Should I? I mean." I wave my right hand. "I mean, it's cliché, but maybe it's a trope for a reason."

Momma gestures to Ma, who steps forward.

"Well," she begins. "I think you should take a shower and get your thoughts in order. Eat a banana, you know the potassium—"

"Will help with the cramps, I got it," I finish for her while heading toward the bathroom.

But even while I scrub my skin until it's pink and raw—the soothing smell of my coconut shower gel filling my nose—I can't stop thinking about Luca kissing me.

And how much I wish it had never happened.

Once I'm out of the shower and dressed in leggings and a pale purple tunic, I curl up on my bed. Lasagna curls up on my stomach, and I wonder if she knows that her body heat is helping me relax. She wobbles back and forth, giving a dainty meow. "Thank you." Scratching her between the ears, I fumble for my phone next to my pillow.

Joy (5:01 p.m.): Luca kissed me.

Valentina (5:01 p.m.): WHAT?! 😮

Yasmine (5:01 p.m.): HE DID?! 😮

Yasmine (5:02 p.m.): We'll be right down.

A few minutes later, Valentina and Yasmine are at my bedroom door. Yasmine has changed out of her school uniform into a pair of jeans and a bright pink sweater patterned with hearts, Valentina, a pair of galaxy-print leggings and a NASA hoodie.

"He kissed you?!" Yasmine says. Her matching heart earrings—the plastic kind filled with pink sequins—move as she and Val both sit on my bed, with me in the middle.

"Did he say"—Valentina pushes her glasses farther up her nose—"anything?"

"Yeah." I adjust my glasses. "He did, actually." Lasagna moves to my lap, and I give her a quick scratch between her ears. "He told me that he has feelings for me, and that's why he's been so off about me going to CIB." My eyes flit to the top of Lasagna's head, and I focus on the small stripes there. "You were right."

I'm expecting Valentina and Yasmine to glance at each

other. The kind couples who've been together for years use to communicate. Theirs would be triumphant—happy that they knew Luca was attracted to me before I had a clue.

Except, they just look at me, their faces scrunched up in thought.

"And then he just"—Valentina tucks her right leg under her left—"kissed you?"

"Yeah." I nod, my shoulders crumpling.

"So, he's afraid," Yasmine says. "But instead of actually talking to us about it, he just vomits all of this to you instead?"

"I mean," Valentina begins, "remember how silly I was when I gave you Caldwell Cupid's letter? Maybe we should give him a break."

"Yeah, but I kissed you," Yasmine says. "After you told me how you felt. You didn't kiss me out of nowhere. He shouldn't have put that on you, Joy."

"I know," I murmur, rubbing my throat again. "But it's just so complicated. It's not that I—I don't love Luca or anything. I do love him. Just like I love the two of you. But not the way he wants me to love him."

"Don't get that in your head," Valentina tells me bracingly. "You can only love people the way you love them. You can't make yourself feel differently."

"Why not?" I murmur. "It might be nice to be with someone. I *want* to fall in love."

"You'll find someone you actually want to kiss," Valentina says.

"All the way in California." Yasmine sighs dreamily. "That's a way better love story than yours and Luca's is."

"Oh yeah, it's a scientific fact," Valentina adds. "Trust me. I'm a future science teacher."

CHAPTER TWENTY-ONE

NATHANIEL

I have a coughing fit the instant I lie down on my blue bedspread. I managed to take off my blazer, but I'm still in my school pants, white button-down, and tie.

Rolling over on my side to face the window, I try to prop myself up onto my elbow, coughing into my blanket and begging my asthma to stop.

"Nathaniel?" Franny's voice asks.

I roll over onto my other side to see my sister standing in the doorway of my bedroom, dressed in a chunky purple sweater and jeans.

"What are you doing home?" I croak.

"I just visited Natalie." She smiles a little. "She's doing well."

"That's great," I say.

"It doesn't seem like you are." Her brow furrows, her smile slipping. "Let me take a look at you."

"Franny." Sighing rattles my lungs. "I'm fine."

She holds up one finger and disappears down the stairs, returning a minute later with her red medical bag, gloves already on her hands.

After Franny listens to my heart and lungs, she tucks her stethoscope around her neck before grabbing a penlight. "Open your mouth and say 'ahh' for me."

Even doing that hurts. Franny knits her brow. "Your throat is red." She gets a thermometer from her bag, putting it under my tongue. A few seconds later, it beeps, and she takes it from my mouth to read the results. "You have a temperature of one hundred and one. Fever, coughing, sore throat." She tuts. "No wonder you feel so bad."

My chest goes warm. It's nice to have someone take care of you. You'd think that would be common in this house, but I can't remember the last time either of my parents cared for me this way.

Franny takes off her gloves, throwing them away in my small garbage can under my desk. "Let me get you a cold compress," she says. She flits out of my room, returning a moment later with a wet washcloth that she lays across my forehead.

"I can't believe you went to school like this. You need to rest." She sits in my desk chair, swiveling it around. "Not to mention you could have gotten other people sick. You know better than that."

"Every day is important." I settle underneath my blanket,

leaning back against my pillows, relying on them and my headboard to keep me propped up. "My school takes attendance into account for valedictorian."

Franny makes a noise that's somewhere between disgust and annoyance. "Your school is so elitist that if you get sick you can't receive honors?" She clucks her tongue. "What an ableist fucking policy. I ought to give them a piece of my mind." She drums her fingers on the arms of my chair. "I swear, if Natalie goes to that school, I will be joining the PTA and writing scathing critiques."

"Does that mean you're thinking about staying here?" I ask, making sure my washcloth doesn't slip down my face.

"It's possible." Franny's tongue pokes out of the corner of her mouth. "I've always loved New York. The only reason I left was because of Richard, after all." She falls quiet, shrugging. "I was young and impulsive. I thought, 'He's a handsome surgeon, what could go wrong?'"

"Does he . . ." My voice trails off into a wheeze, and Franny hands me my backpack so I can retrieve my inhaler. "Does he know about Natalie being born early and everything?" I ask after the second dose of medicine.

"He does," Franny replies quietly. "I told him. Richard never wanted children. And I thought my patients would be enough, but when I realized that I was pregnant, I knew that I wanted to be a mom so badly." She smiles to herself, looking at me. "My daughter is the best thing in my life. If I gave birth in

Tennessee, I wouldn't have had the support system I did that night, you know. We didn't really know anyone there. I'd have been alone. Luckily, I had you."

"You're welcome." I smile back at her.

"Warren and Everett tell me you want to be an ob-gyn?" She smiles again when I nod. "So, what does that mean for you? Do you think you'll stay in California?"

"No," I say immediately. She seems so excited about my future that I don't have the heart to tell her that the California Institute of Biology is no longer an option for me. "I don't see myself living there permanently. I like seasons too much."

"Seasons, or someone?" Franny chuckles, her eyes bright.

"Excuse me?" I'm actually grateful for the coughing fit that happens next so I can cover up the surprise of a question I already know the answer to.

"Well," Franny says thoughtfully. "I know you aren't up at all hours of the night writing to yourself."

My mouth falls open. Air creaks across my lips and a coldness floods my back as I realize that I may never write to Joy again. "How'd you know?"

"My room is right next to yours," she says. "I hear you typing, and I see the light from your monitor under your door when I get up during the night."

"Oh." I blow out a breath. "I'm sorry about that."

"Don't be." She shakes her head. "I'm just glad you've got

something—or someone—other than school. It's healthy for you to have that balance."

"I don't have it anymore." I sigh, looking up at the ceiling to avoid her eyes. "I thought I did. But I ruined everything."

"Everything?" Franny asks gently. "Come on now, you're being dramatic."

I bring my gaze to hers. There's a wrinkle between her brows. "Considering who our mother is, are you surprised?"

"No, I guess not." She chuckles a little bit. "Do you want to tell me what happened?"

"We had a fight." I shrug. "And I don't think she wants to talk to me anymore."

"Well." Franny gets to her feet. "I'm sorry you and Joy had an argument, but—"

"Hey." I blink at her. "I never said—"

"No more talking." Franny fluffs my pillows. "I'll make chicken and noodles for dinner. The broth and veggies should help. In the meantime, I'll bring you a snack and some ibuprofen for the fever. After you take the medicine, you get some rest while I cook. Doctor's orders."

She leaves my bedroom, the stairs creaking with each step as she heads for the kitchen. I lean back against my pillows. A sigh melts into a wheeze just as my phone chimes with a new email notification.

To: Caldwell Cupid (cupid@caldwellcupid.com)

From: Joy Corvi (joy.corvi@caldwell.edu)

Date: March 27, 5:25 p.m.

Subject: Luca

Dear Cupid,

Luca kissed me.

I wish I were here to spin you a dramatic tale like in one of your romance novels. I wish I felt something cliché during the kiss.

Fireworks.

Butterflies.

The first bit of sun on your face in summertime, when school is done for the year, and you have weeks of free time ahead of you.

But I didn't feel any of those things.

I just wanted it to be over.

I wish I did have feelings for Luca. All of this would be much less complicated.

Sincerely,

Joy

To: Joy Corvi (joy.corvi@caldwell.edu)
From: Caldwell Cupid (cupid@caldwellcupid.com)
Date: March 28, 9:27 a.m.
Subject: RE: Luca

Dear Joy,
It would be less complicated. But I don't think it would be special.

Please never feel bad about not reciprocating someone's feelings. Whom a person chooses to kiss—if they choose to kiss anyone at all—is their choice.

The thing about romance is, it only works when everyone wants it to.

Sincerely,
Cupid

To: Caldwell Cupid (cupid@caldwellcupid.com)

From: Joy Corvi (joy.corvi@caldwell.edu)

Date: March 29, 10:10 a.m.

Subject: Liking Someone

Dear Cupid,

But can't love grow? Plenty of people fall in love with their best friends.

Sincerely,

Joy

To: Joy Corvi (joy.corvi@caldwell.edu)

From: Caldwell Cupid (cupid@caldwellcupid.com)

Date: March 29, 11:30 p.m.

Subject: RE: Liking Someone

Dear Joy,

I suppose that is true. Sometimes friendships grow into love. But it happens naturally, it isn't forced. I know how that feels.

Sincerely,

Cupid

To: Caldwell Cupid (cupid@caldwellcupid.com)

From: Joy Corvi (joy.corvi@caldwell.edu)

Date: April 1, 3:00 p.m.

Subject: RE: RE: Liking Someone

Dear Cupid,

How does it feel?

Sincerely,

Joy

To: Joy Corvi (joy.corvi@caldwell.edu)

From: Caldwell Cupid (cupid@caldwellcupid.com)

Date: April 2, 9:00 a.m.

Subject: My Experience

Dear Joy,

The first time I felt it was when I kissed a boy I had been friends with after school.

We kept kissing on the subway, and I remember being grateful for how packed the train was. No one paid us any mind. You have to love New Yorkers, never fazed by anything on the subway.

I don't think I ever fell in love with him, but it was so nice to let that friendship grow for a little while. I was comfortable with him; I felt safe. He accepted me for who I am.

In fact, I just got an email from someone who likes him requesting that I write a love letter to him.

Love works in mysterious ways, I suppose.

Sincerely,

Cupid

To: Caldwell Cupid (cupid@caldwellcupid.com)

From: Joy Corvi (joy.corvi@caldwell.edu)

Date: April 2, 10:00 p.m.

Subject: You

Dear Cupid,

I guess the only time I ever feel that comfortable is while I'm writing to you.

Sincerely,

Joy

To: Joy Corvi (joy.corvi@caldwell.edu)

From: Caldwell Cupid (cupid@caldwellcupid.com)

Date: April 3, 1:00 a.m.

Subject: RE: You

Dear Joy,

I feel the same way.

Sincerely,

Cupid

To: Caldwell Cupid (cupid@caldwellcupid.com)

From: Joy Corvi (joy.corvi@caldwell.edu)

Date: April 3, 1:10 a.m.

Subject: Us

Dear Cupid,

Maybe this could grow?

Sincerely,

Joy

To: Joy Corvi (joy.corvi@caldwell.edu)

From: Caldwell Cupid (cupid@caldwellcupid.com)

Date: April 3, 1:45 a.m.

Subject: RE: Us

Dear Joy,

I think it already has.

Yours,

Cupid

To: Caldwell Cupid (cupid@caldwellcupid.com)

From: Joy Corvi (joy.corvi@caldwell.edu)

Date: April 3, 2:00 a.m.

Subject: RE: RE: Us

Dear Cupid,

What do we do now?

Yours,

Joy

To: Joy Corvi (joy.corvi@caldwell.edu)

From: Caldwell Cupid (cupid@caldwellcupid.com)

Date: April 3, 2:05 a.m.

Subject: RE: RE: RE: Us

Dear Joy,

I'm not sure yet. Let me think about that.

Yours,

Cupid

CHAPTER TWENTY-TWO

JOY

Cupid likes me.

And I like them.

CHAPTER TWENTY-THREE

NATHANIEL

Joy likes me.

Or rather, Joy likes Cupid.

Right now, Joy hates me.

To: Caldwell Cupid (cupid@caldwellcupid.com)

From: Luca Sapienti (luca.sapienti@caldwell.edu)

Date: April 5, 7:00 p.m.

Subject: Joy

Dear Cupid,

I kissed Joy just before spring break. She pulled away from me and wants to forget it ever happened. And we have.

At least around each other.

But I don't want to forget. How do I get her to kiss me again?

Luca

To: Luca Sapienti (luca.sapienti@caldwell.edu)

From: Caldwell Cupid (cupid@caldwellcupid.com)

Date: April 5, 7:10 p.m.

Subject: RE: Joy

Luca,

Joy can kiss whomever she wants. You can't convince her to kiss you again.

She's far too smart to fall for any of your games, anyway.

(Saved to drafts)

CHAPTER TWENTY-FOUR
JOY

Cupid and I haven't emailed since confessing our feelings to each other.

But the very idea that I like someone is enough to buoy me the entire first full week back from spring break.

That is, until just before the elementary school science night at P.S. 333, when I'm distracted by something that has nothing to do with late-night letters or my suddenly burgeoning romantic life.

"So, Joy." Valentina grins broadly as Mr. Baumann leads us toward the gym, holding his wife's hand. They're talking in low voices and can't seem to go long without nudging each other's shoulders. "Are you ready for tomorrow?"

"Yeah." I smile, my cheeks warming. I know being the vice president of the Caldwell Science Society and vying for valedictorian speaks to the contrary, but I don't really like to be the center of attention.

Still, you don't turn eighteen every day.

"What's tomorrow?" Declan asks as he, Vikram, and Nathaniel enter through the lobby doors behind us.

"My birthday," Nathaniel and I say in unison.

Wait.

We spin around to face each other, fast enough that I somehow manage to smack my elbow into my side. "Your birthday." The first two words Nathaniel and I have spoken to each other all week. Since the Caldwell Science Society meeting before spring break, actually.

"Is April eleventh." Nathaniel nods.

"S-Same as mine." I nod, too, and both of our eyes narrow.

"Nathaniel!" Vikram says, breaking our staring contest. "Your birthday is tomorrow?! He's always kept his birthday a secret," he explains to me, Valentina, Yasmine, and Luca. "Doesn't want us to go all out or get him any gifts."

Declan spins himself around so that he starts walking backward. "I've never even been able to bake you a birthday cake, you bastard!"

"I . . ." Nathaniel runs a hand first through his tousled blond curls, then down his face until his chin is in his palm. Something's different. I've never seen him *embarrassed* before. And right now, his face is nearly as red as his cashmere sweater. "Well, because I've . . ."

His voice trails off when we enter the gym. Half the space is taken up by science fair projects: Volcanoes. Solar system models. Even a project on tardigrades.

The other half is set up for our demonstration of paper helicopters. A group of kids and adults seated in cushioned folding chairs, waiting for us in front of a plum-colored backdrop. The words THE CALDWELL SCIENCE SOCIETY are hung across it in silver bubble letters, framing a simple, elevated wooden platform.

Noise presses against both sides of my head, and I'm itching to put my hands over my ears to block it out, but I force them to stay at my sides instead. To distract myself, I glance at Nathaniel again and see that he's not focused on the science fair, or our presentation area, or the noise.

He's talking to a blond man who could only be his brother, a redheaded woman, and two small children who look a lot like Nathaniel.

"Uncle Nathaniel!" one of the kids squeals. She runs up to him, throwing her arms around his waist in a hug.

"Hi, Uncle Nathaniel!" the boy says, waving.

"Hi." Nathaniel smiles at his niece and nephew. "Ready to learn about paper helicopters?"

After dazzling a group of elementary schoolers with the wonders of paper and aerodynamics, we thank everyone for coming before leaving P.S. 333. As we walk outside, all of us are yawning and tired.

"What were you about to say?" I ask. "Before we walked into the gym?"

"Yeah, can we please get back to the discussion of how you've been lying to your *best friends* about your birthday?" Declan adds.

"Is Party City still open?" Vikram asks. "Let's get supplies so we can celebrate!"

"We got Joy's yesterday," Valentina says. I'm looking in front of me so I don't accidentally trip on the sidewalk—because cerebral palsy makes tripping over anything incredibly easy—but I can hear her smile. "We throw a themed one for her every year. Just a little one in her apartment. Last year's was my favorite; it was beach themed. Even managed to get a kiddie pool in her living room!" Valentina's laugh echoes up to the ambient light around us. "We filled it with water and Swedish Fish."

"I—I don't know how you did all that without me noticing," I say.

"Your moms helped," Valentina chuckles. "They hid the pool under their bed for three weeks."

"Oh my God!" I giggle. "That—"

"Sounds amazing," Nathaniel murmurs, marvel thick in his voice. "I've never had a birthday party," he admits sheepishly, causing all of us to look at him. But his gaze flits between his two best friends, both of whom are staring back with concerned eyes.

"You've *never* had a birthday party?" Declan murmurs. "Ever?"

"Nope." Nathaniel shakes his head. "My parents were always too busy to plan ahead for those kinds of things. At least, by the time I was born. They made sure we did stuff, like go to the Bronx Zoo or something. But I've never—"

"Had a cake?" Vikram asks. "Had people sing 'Happy Birthday' terribly off-key? Blown out candles? Made a wish? Balloons?!"

Nathaniel shakes his head and shrugs. My heart sinks. Every kid should get a party. The cold April wind blows back my bangs, and I steel myself against the muscle spasm that courses from my left shoulder down to my fingertips.

"Well, we need to fix that," I find myself saying. Nathaniel turns his gaze to mine, his eyes bright under the streetlights. "W-Would you like to, um . . ." My voice fades in my throat. "Celebrate our birthday together?" I look at Vikram and Declan next. "You two can come, too, of course."

"I'm already baking your cake," Declan adds happily, gesturing behind us where Luca is standing, silent as I have ever seen him. "Luca gave me the design."

"Joy," Nathaniel murmurs. "Do you mean it? You really want me to come to your birthday party?"

"Yes." I nod. "Besides, it'll be *our* birthday party. You should have at least one before college."

"Thank you." Nathaniel smiles at me, his dimples popping. "So." He looks at Yasmine and Valentina. "What's the theme for tomorrow?"

"Oh, we never tell the birthday kid before the party," Yasmine says, grinning at him. "It's a surprise."

To: Joy Corvi (joy.corvi@caldwell.edu)

From: Caldwell Cupid (cupid@caldwellcupid.com)

Date: April 10, 11:11 p.m.

Subject: Love Letter #1

Dear Joy,

I like you.

We don't know each other beyond our keystrokes. Beyond our words. Beyond our sentences. Beyond reading each other's words at all hours of the night.

And yet.

I like you.

That's one of the marvels of romance, isn't it?

Yours,

Cupid

To: Caldwell Cupid (cupid@caldwellcupid.com)
From: Joy Corvi (joy.corvi@caldwell.edu)
Date: April 11, 12:02 a.m.
Subject: RE: Love Letter #1

Dear Cupid,

Love works in strange ways. You should know that better than anyone. I learned it from you.

And though you know who I am, I have yet to learn your identity.

If we ever do meet in person, I hope you wouldn't look at me strangely. I hope you wouldn't stare at my left hand when it fists or when I raise it. I hope you wouldn't be overly gentle with me because I stutter. I hope you wouldn't think I was strange when sometimes sounds I've heard my entire life become too much for my ears.

I hope you would just see me. For all that I am.

And now I need to ask this before I lose my courage: Who are you?

Yours,

Joy

CHAPTER TWENTY-FIVE

NATHANIEL

Both of my parents are gone when I wake up on my eighteenth birthday, but Franny makes celebratory bacon, egg, and cheeses for breakfast as Natalie cuddles against her chest, secured in her floral-patterned wrap.

My niece has been home from the hospital for a week now and Franny has been with her constantly.

"Happy birthday!" Franny sings, placing my breakfast plate in front of me.

"So." Daniel reaches across the dining table to hold my sister's hand as we eat. He's been staying over a lot, when Mother and Father work overnight shifts. "Any big birthday plans?"

Franny plucks a piece of egg-soaked bacon from her plate, popping it into her mouth. "You're eighteen now," she says. "You should do something special."

"I am." I smile down at my breakfast sandwich before continuing. "My . . . friends are throwing a birthday party."

"They are?" Franny squeals, hugging Natalie as she grins. "That's such big news! I've never had one, you know."

"Excuse me?" Daniel squeezes my sister's hand. "Baby, you've never had—"

"You know what?" My sister gets to her feet to swoop across the table and kiss her boyfriend. "My birthday is on November second. We can talk about it then." She kisses him again. "But speaking of big news." Franny's eyes go wide, and she looks like she is about to burst.

"What big news?" I ask.

"Arthur is proposing to Everett!" she whispers, barely able to contain her excitement.

My mouth falls open. *"He is?"*

"Yes!" Franny squeals. "He plans to propose on May sixteenth, the day they met. At the Dog and Moon, where they had their first date!"

"Our brother is getting engaged?" I whisper, beaming.

"He is!" Franny polishes off her sandwich. "But don't you dare say anything, okay?"

"Never!" I finish my sandwich, wiping the yolk from my fingers. "I wouldn't ruin the surprise."

"Which reminds me!" Franny gets to her feet, practically dancing out of the kitchen. She returns a minute later with a red bag covered in party hats and confetti with the words HAPPY BIRTHDAY! printed on it in silver letters. "Presents!"

My cheeks hurt from smiling as I accept the bag and take out the tissue paper. I pull out two giant textbooks. *An Introduction to Obstetrics & Gynecology* and *The Labor & Delivery Manual*.

"Thank you." The words are tight in my throat, squeezing tears from my eyes.

"Oh, Nathaniel." As much as she can with a baby on her chest, Franny gives me a hug. "You're welcome."

"Textbooks?" Daniel asks, confused.

"It's kind of a family tradition." Franny shrugs.

"You guys sure are an interesting family." Daniel smiles. "If you ever need help once you begin to study, I'm always available."

"Thank you." I smile at him as I grab a piece of paper towel to wipe my eyes.

"C'mon now, no more tears," Franny says, looking at me. "You go upstairs and get ready for your birthday party."

"No." Declan smirks as he, Vikram, and I enter the elevator, heading up to Joy's apartment. He glances down at the frosted case he held throughout the entire ride on the Q train here. "You're not allowed to see your birthday cake yet."

"I'm not marrying the cake," I whine. "Why can't I see it?"

"Because that'll give away the theme." Vikram smooths

down his bisexual pride T-shirt. "I know this is your first time, just lean into it. It's fun!"

I sigh, leaning against the elevator and blowing a blond curl off my forehead. "Fine," I say, my smirk giving way to a snort so embarrassing that I cover my mouth and nose.

"It's okay to be excited, you know," Declan says cheekily.

Soon, we reach Joy's unit, and I knock on the door. Just once. Like I'm afraid to touch it more than necessary. Like I'm afraid she'll know from the knock on the door who I really am.

My ears perk up at the sound of footsteps, and I straighten my spine, willing my heart to return to its place in my ribs instead of making a new home for itself in between my ears.

"Calm down," I whisper to myself.

"Calm down?" Vikram repeats, nudging me. "Are you nervous?"

"No," I say quickly. "I'm—"

"Nathaniel." I swallow my sentence at the sound of Joy's voice. She's standing at the threshold, wearing a pale green dress with capped sleeves and the same floral headband from Valentine's Day. Her left hand is fisted at her breast, and she's rocking back and forth on the balls of her feet like I do.

"Joy." I squeeze her name from my chest, a warmth coursing through me as she smiles. "Hi. Happy birthday."

"T-To us," she replies.

"Indeed." I nod, trying my best to smile back at her.

She leads us down the hall and into the living room. There

are dinosaurs everywhere—cutouts, stuffed animals, and at the center of the room is a full blanket fort, made up entirely of different dinosaur-patterned throw blankets.

"Welcome to your birthday party!" Valentina and Yasmine grin as they peek their heads out from the blanket fort, each of them wearing a party hat patterned with green metallic dinosaur silhouettes.

"It's dinosaur-themed!" Luca says from the kitchen as Yasmine presents us with party hats.

"We'll be marathoning *The Land Before Time* movies," Valentina says. "My older brother used to love them when he was a kid."

"My brothers and sister, too," I add.

"Cillian, too," Declan chimes in from the kitchen. "So, they have to either be cinematic masterpieces or disasters. Either way, it should be a good time."

"Okay, but first . . . Cake!" Joy says from next to me. She bounces on the balls of her feet again, her cheeks pink. "I love sweets, so I always have them first at these parties."

Joy laughs when we walk into the kitchen to see a stegosaurus cake sitting on the counter. "It's huge! How did you get this here on the subway?"

"Perseverance," I mutter, glancing at her. My cheeks warm when we smile at each other again.

Everyone sings "Happy Birthday" and we dig in. It's delicious; I wouldn't expect anything less from Declan. The frosting is chocolate; the cake itself is this soft, delicate raspberry, with raspberry filling piped between the layers.

"H-How's your first birthday cake?" Joy asks, her eyes gleaming. She really does love sweets. For a split second, I wonder if her eyes look the same when she's sitting in front of her computer screen writing to Cupid or as she's reading the letters I send to her.

"Nate?" Luca prompts, making me bristle. "She asked you a question."

"Oh," I splutter. "It-It's amazing." Swallowing my mouthful of cake, I add, "Thank you."

"Nathaniel," Joy corrects Luca while she smiles at me in such a gentle way that it makes my heart crack. "Let's see how you feel after I'm named valedictorian tomorrow."

I nearly spit out my second bite of cake.

I'd been so wrapped up in everything going on that I completely forgot that our four-year-long battle will come to an end tomorrow.

"And may the best of us win," I murmur instead, marveling at how her entire body softens at my words. "No matter who it is."

To: Joy Corvi (joy.corvi@caldwell.edu)

From: Caldwell Cupid (cupid@caldwellcupid.com)

Date: April 11, 10:20 p.m.

Subject: Love Letter #2

Dear Joy,

I have to admit that I'm nervous about telling you who I am over email. We've been writing to each other, opening our hearts to each other, for months. What if I'm not the person you imagine me to be?

I've seen you around at school, I know how beautiful you are, how kind you are, and how intelligent you are. Things I already knew have only become clearer in all these letters.

And while I promise that I see you for all that you are—your cerebral palsy, your queer identity, everything—I'm nervous to put that weight on your shoulders when it comes to me.

However, I know you deserve to know who I am. I've wanted to tell you, for months. But that is something that I need to do outside of these letters we've written to each other.

Would you like to meet in person?

Yours,

Cupid

CHAPTER TWENTY-SIX

JOY

Cupid wants to meet.

They want us to emerge from behind our computers and phones. To become a part of each other's lives beyond the words and letters and sentences that make up our emails. Beyond the very reason we developed feelings for each other.

Hiding my phone behind my laptop in AP English, I reread that part of Cupid's most recent love letter:

I know you deserve to know who I am . . . Would you like to meet in person?

My tongue presses up into my soft palate as I mouth a reply to myself. I do want to meet them. Their letters have become more than advice from the academy's resident romance expert. I'm not sure they were ever just that. Was I, on some level, hoping to connect with someone who views romance the same way I do?

"Joy Corvi and Nathaniel Wright." Even though I've been waiting to hear Principal Mason's voice, it still makes a muscle spasm travel from the crook of my elbow to my fingertips. "Please come to the main office at once."

I rise to my feet so fast that my knees smack into the underside of my desk.

"Shit," I hiss as pain pings up my legs.

"Are you okay, Joy?" Valentina whispers from her seat beside me so as not to disturb Miss Neilson's lecture on *Macbeth*.

"Yeah," I whisper back, swinging my backpack onto my shoulders. "I-I'm fine. I-I'll see you after school?"

"To celebrate," Yasmine says from her seat in front of me. She turns around, grinning. "We promise."

Blowing out a breath from in between my lips, I head up to the front of the room. Miss Neilson nods at me as I leave. I square my shoulders and shrug off the pain radiating through my body.

Still, as I limp to the main office, my anxiety trades places with my muscle spasms and hurt knees. From physical to mental. Different, but on the same level. I know that both Nathaniel and I have worked as hard as each other for this opportunity, this honor.

But I also know that I'm immediately underestimated whenever anyone meets me for the first time. I can see how their lips move when they're preparing to slow down their speech. Their slow blink as they try to process the reality of a disabled person who's capable of more than their preconceived notions have taught them. The quick glances when my left hand is raised at my breast when I'm simply out in public with my moms. How eyes shift to Ma or Momma when a question is asked about me, as if I'm not actually there and cannot possibly answer for myself.

Nathaniel could never understand. People actually want to look at him; they expect him to be smart. They hang on his words.

The world wants people like Nathaniel.

They don't want people like me.

But if I am named valedictorian, then perhaps—

"Hi, Joy."

Nathaniel's voice startles me. I'd walked all the way to the main office, so completely lost in my own thoughts that I didn't think to watch where I was walking. I'm lucky I didn't trip over myself.

Instead, I walked right into Nathaniel.

"H-Hi, Nathaniel." My reply is nearly lost in my throat, but thankfully, we didn't come to the main office to talk to each other.

We came to see who has won what we've both fought so hard for.

The secretary leads us into Principal Mason's office, a

surprisingly sparse place in a school so elite. An oak desk, a purple chair I'm almost positive she's required to sit in, a computer, and two purple chairs that sit in the middle of the room. The silver walls are clean, same as the desk. Not even so much as a succulent next to her computer mouse or a diploma displayed behind her.

"Joy, Nathaniel." Principal Mason's voice is as crisp as her silver pantsuit and brown curls. "Welcome. Please sit." I sink gratefully into the seat. It wasn't that long of a distance to walk from Miss Neilson's room to here, but when my muscles are tight, even taking a few steps is painful.

"Now," she begins. "Both of you know why I called you here. You are two of the brightest students in the history of Caldwell Preparatory Academy, and you should be proud of your achievements here within its halls. It has been an honor to watch you both flourish in academia these past four years. And I have no doubt that you both will continue to do so at the California Institute of Biology in the fall."

Her praise makes my cheeks warm. I glance over at Nathaniel and see that the color is high in his cheeks, too. "Thank you," we chorus.

"You're very welcome." Principal Mason clears her throat. "With that being said, however, there can only be one valedictorian and one salutatorian. And I'm sure you're eager to see which one of you has received which honor. Are you ready?"

"Yes." Nathaniel and I glance at each other again. The

color is still in his cheeks, and I'm sure mine are still pink.

Before I can think about it, I find my spidery left fingers lacing through Nathaniel's, and to my surprise, he squeezes them. I squeeze his fingers back as Principal Mason folds her hands.

"Very well," she says, looking between us. "Nathaniel, you are valedictorian. Joy, you are salutatorian." She smiles. "Congratulations."

Her words make my muscles seize throughout my whole body, including my fingers weaved through Nathaniel's. My throat tightens as it forces emotions to stay down in my chest instead of springing to the surface. I slip my hand from Nathaniel's and get to my feet before I burst into tears in Principal Mason's office.

"Thank you," I say, not able to bring myself to meet Nathaniel's eyes. "Nathaniel, I—I—" Without finishing my sentence, I stumble out of the room, through the main office, and into the hallway, lurching forward on my palsied left foot.

"Joy." Nathaniel's voice fills my ears. Even though I know I should congratulate him and leave, I turn around anyway. His face has gone pale.

"What?" My own voice cracks on its way out. My fingernails dig into my palm, and I'm grateful for the flash of pain that brings to keep me from crying. "You w-want to console me or something?"

"No." Nathaniel puts his hands in the pockets of his purple

pants. "I . . . just wanted to make sure you were okay."

"Oh." The word wobbles in my mouth. "I'm . . ." I blink, shoving tears away as they roll down my cheeks. "I need to be alone right now. I—I don't want to cry in front of you." I pivot on my right heel, swiping at my face again.

"We both worked so hard for this," Nathaniel murmurs. "The two most intelligent people either of us knows?" Echoes, memories of our conversation from months ago flood my head. "Of course, one of us was bound to be upset."

"You think I don't know that?" I can barely hear myself speak through the sob that chokes the words, let alone know if Nathaniel can hear me. "I-I've *always* had to push myself at this school, you know. T-To prove to myself I'm more than wh-what people see. And it—it wasn't enough."

"Joy—"

"Still," I whisper, "you deserve to win."

"You deserved to win, too," Nathaniel whispers back.

I nod. Stretching up on my tiptoes, I kiss his cheek, just as he'd kissed mine on Christmas Eve. "Congratulations."

I walk out of the building, grateful for the throngs of students doing the same thing so I melt between them easily.

When I get home, Ma is sitting on the couch in the living room, a glass bottle of cider on the end table, a pair of knitting needles in her hands, and a pile of pastel rainbow yarn in her lap. She knit my asexual pride scarf when I came out in my sophomore year, but I have no idea what she's working on now.

"Hi, Joy." Ma smiles at me, putting her needles down. "How was—"

I start bawling before she finishes her sentence. Big, gasping breaths that make my chest shudder and tighten at once. I cough out sobs while hot tears stream down my cheeks.

"Joy Elise." Ma wraps me up in her arms. She smells like vanilla and sugar, which probably means our cookie jar in the kitchen has been properly restocked. "Do you wanna tell me what's wrong?" Her voice is hard. She's not inclined to speak softly; instead, she shows her love through actions, like putting her knitting down because I burst into tears.

"I'm not valedictorian," I hiccup, tasting the salt from my tears. I sniff before continuing. "Nathaniel beat me."

"Joy—"

"He deserves it," I murmur, drying my eyes with the sleeve of my blazer. "Of course he does. It—It hurts, because . . . I worked just as hard as he did."

"I know you did." Ma squeezes me before stepping back. "And I know how badly you wanted this. I know much you've studied. Not just this year, either, but all your life. The moment you . . ." She purses her lips as her voice cracks a little, her dark brown bangs falling across her forehead. We look nothing alike, and yet our bangs drape the same way. "The moment you were old enough to understand what I did for a living, you wanted to follow in my footsteps. The toy stethoscope when you were a little girl. The college textbooks you started reading as soon as you could." She sighs gently, which warms my stomach. My copy of *The Labor & Delivery Manual* sits on a shelf above my desk; I still remember how excited I was to receive it as a birthday present.

"Sweetheart, you're salutatorian," she continues. "That is *such* an accomplishment; you realize that, don't you?" I nod. "Exactly. Momma and I are so proud of you. And you are *still* bound be a brilliant NICU nurse someday. Understand?"

"Yes, ma'am," I murmur as she kisses my forehead.

"Good," she replies. "Now you go relax."

Valentina (7:05 p.m.): Hey, how are you feeling? Can we come over?

Joy (7:07 p.m.): I just want to be alone.

Valentina (7:08 p.m.): Please don't shut us out. We just want to be there for you.

Joy (7:11 p.m.): I know. You're good friends. But I'm just tired, and really upset.

Luca (7:13 p.m.): Ok, well, we are outside your door. How about we just give you some quick hugs.

Luca (7:13 p.m.): And then we'll go. No words. Just big hugs?

Joy (7:14 p.m.): Okay. I'd like that.

To: Caldwell Cupid (cupid@caldwellcupid.com)

From: Joy Corvi (joy.corvi@caldwell.edu)

Date: April 12, 11:11 p.m.

Subject: Valedictorian

Dear Cupid,

It's been a hard day. I'm not valedictorian. I know Nathaniel deserves this. He is the smartest person I know.

But is it okay to say that I also feel bad for myself? I know I should be proud to be salutatorian . . . But I still feel an ache in my chest. I wanted this so bad.

Yours,

Joy

P.S. I would really like to meet in person.

To: Joy Corvi (joy.corvi@caldwell.edu)
From: Caldwell Cupid (cupid@caldwellcupid.com)
Date: April 14, 12:33 a.m.
Subject: RE: Valedictorian

Dear Joy,

I don't want you to hurt.

If I could be there with you, I would hold you, with one arm around your shoulders, the other around your waist. I would cradle you against my chest, kissing the top of your head every so often just to let you know that I'm there.

Would that be enough?

Yours,

Cupid

To: Caldwell Cupid (cupid@caldwellcupid.com)

From: Joy Corvi (joy.corvi@caldwell.edu)

Date: April 25, 3:00 p.m.

Subject: RE: RE: Valedictorian

Dear Cupid,

It would be more than enough.

Yours,

Joy

To: Joy Corvi (joy.corvi@caldwell.edu)

From: Caldwell Cupid (cupid@caldwellcupid.com)

Date: April 25, 3:30 p.m.

Subject: RE: RE: RE: Valedictorian

Dear Joy,

I would love to kiss you.

Yours,

Cupid

To: Caldwell Cupid (cupid@caldwellcupid.com)

From: Joy Corvi (joy.corvi@caldwell.edu)

Date: April 25, 11:00 p.m.

Subject: RE: RE: RE: RE: Valedictorian

Dear Cupid,

Why?

Yours,

Joy

To: Joy Corvi (joy.corvi@caldwell.edu)

From: Caldwell Cupid (cupid@caldwellcupid.com)

Date: April 26, 12:12 a.m.

Subject: Love Letter #3

Dear Joy,

Because I think I have fallen in love with you.

Yours,

Cupid

To: Caldwell Cupid (cupid@caldwellcupid.com)

From: Joy Corvi (joy.corvi@caldwell.edu)

Date: April 26, 12:50 a.m.

Subject: RE: Love Letter #3

Dear Cupid,

I think I have fallen in love with you, too.

Yours,

Joy

To: Joy Corvi (joy.corvi@caldwell.edu)

From: Caldwell Cupid (cupid@caldwellcupid.com)

Date: April 26, 1:30 a.m.

Subject: A Promposal

Dear Joy,

Do you want to go to prom with me?

Yours,

Cupid

To: Caldwell Cupid (cupid@caldwellcupid.com)

From: Joy Corvi (joy.corvi@caldwell.edu)

Date: April 26, 1:31 a.m.

Subject: RE: A Promposal

Dear Cupid,

Yes.

Yours,

Joy

To: Joy Corvi (joy.corvi@caldwell.edu)

From: Caldwell Cupid (cupid@caldwellcupid.com)

Date: April 26, 1:34 a.m.

Subject: RE: RE: A Promposal

Dear Joy,

Let's meet at the Bethesda Terrace at 6:00 p.m.

Yours,

Cupid

April 26th

Joy (1:35 a.m.): Cupid ask me to prom.

Yasmine (1:36 a.m.): THEY DID?!

Valentina (1:36 a.m.): DID YOU SAY YES?!

Joy (1:36 a.m.): YES, I DID.

Valentina (1:37 a.m.): Not only are you going to MEET Cupid, but you are GOING TO PROM WITH THEM!

Yasmine (1:38 a.m.): We have to go dress shopping.

Yasmine (1:38 a.m.): Except, Val, we can't see each other's dress before prom.

Valentina (1:38 a.m.): Obviously.

Joy (1:40 a.m.): Don't worry. We will keep the mystery alive!

Valentina (1:41 a.m.): And we'll be sure your dress is so cute that Cupid won't know what to do with themself.

CHAPTER TWENTY-SEVEN

JOY

The weeks before prom itself passed in a blur of dress shopping. I was grateful to sink into the world of sequins, tulle, sweetheart necklines, and rainbows of fabric as a distraction. Losing valedictorian still stung, but visiting every single department store in the entirety of Manhattan kept me busy.

My palsied legs hurt at the end of each shopping trip, but it was worth it.

I chose an emerald-green dress with a handkerchief hem, a sweetheart neckline, and sequins scattered throughout the bodice. It matched my fair skin, red hair, freckles, and blue eyes in a way no other piece of clothing ever had before. As a bonus, it highlighted my curves instead of hiding them away.

I felt beautiful sitting in the back of the gray limo my moms rented for us.

"Your dress is the color of the sun and I do love space, so . . ." Valentina muses, pulling Yasmine close.

Valentina decided on a yellow gown with a slit on the side up to her knee. Yasmine chose a gorgeous, strapless red gown that waterfalled down to her ankles.

Luca wore the same fuchsia tuxedo from New Year's Eve and an extremely sour look on his face.

"I'm sorry, but does no one else think that Joy agreeing to go to prom with someone none of us know is weird?" Luca asks.

"I—I mean . . ." I shrug. "It kind of is? B-But I *do* know Cupid. And in getting to know them, I . . ." Closing my eyes, I fold my hands in my lap, my left one scrabbling over my right. ". . . I realized something about myself, too."

"Yeah?" Valentina's voice asks, but she can't pull her eyes away from Yasmine.

"I, uh . . ." I look down at my hands. "I'm panromantic ace."

"Joy!" Valentina and Yasmine reach across the plush limo seats, pulling me into a hug. One that Luca joins, too, his long arms wrapping around us.

"Thank you," Luca murmurs into our tangle of arms and love. "For sharing that with us."

"Of course," I say, smiling when we all break apart. "You're my best friends."

"So." Yasmine grins. "What time are you meeting Cupid?"

"Six," I reply, digging my phone out of a clutch that matches my dress. It's 5:45 p.m.

Just fifteen minutes.

For all its finery and academic elitism, Caldwell Preparatory Academy's senior prom has never been held in some swanky Manhattan ballroom with marble floors and walls made of crystals or something equally ridiculous.

Instead, it's always been in Bethesda Terrace at Central Park.

But even the fairy lights draped around everywhere, twinkling across the surface of Central Park Lake, can't stop my heart from pattering in my chest. The sound travels from my ribs up to my ears, beating in the center of my head. The music from the deejay booth fades away, my own heartbeat becoming all I can hear, all I can concentrate on. To the point that I'm lucky I don't trip over myself.

Though I do stumble across the brick a few times.

Right into Nathaniel, Vikram, Declan, and Eitan Simon, who has been waiting for Declan after Caldwell Science Society meetings for the last few weeks.

"Oh!" I step back, my left hand immediately rising to be at level with my chest. "I-I'm sorry. I didn't—"

"She didn't see where she was going," Luca interjects good-naturedly from beside me.

"Yeah," I murmur, my cheeks flushing. "I—I have a lot on my mind."

"You could say that." Valentina wraps her arm around my waist. "How much longer until you go meet Cupid?"

"Cupid?" Nathaniel repeats. He steps more into the fairy lights. The sleeves of his pink button-down are rolled up to his elbows and his khakis glow. He has the ability to make even the simplest of clothes look as if he's modeling them, and I wonder if that's a conscious choice.

"Wait, hang on." Vikram shakes his head. "You *know* Cupid, Joy?"

"They're the reason we're together," Eitan adds, holding hands with Declan.

"Us too," Yasmine adds, hugging Valentina. "And Joy knows exactly who they are."

"W-Well," I stammer, clearing my throat. "I—I don't know *who* they are. But I . . ." Like I did back in the limo, I close my eyes, filling my chest with breath in the hopes that it'll somehow slow down my heartbeat.

"You what?" Declan asks gently.

"So, you don't know who they are," Vikram says, "but you're meeting them tonight?"

I blow out a breath between my lips. "Yes," I reply. "And I—I know this may seem strange, but I . . ." Opening my eyes, I let the next few words fall off my tongue. "I'm in love with them. Whoever they are."

A collective gasp echoes from everyone around me, and

they each step backward, as though this were a choreographed musical number.

"Well, they must feel the same," Eitan says excitedly. "I mean, they've remained anonymous all this time, and now they are just going to drop the facade. For you! That's huge."

I hadn't thought of it that way. My chest gets even tighter.

"All right, I can't listen to this anymore," Luca almost shouts. "You have no idea what you're talking about." He whips his head in my direction, his eyes narrowed behind his glasses. "You're all being ridiculous. Especially you, Joy."

"What do you mean?" I ask feebly, my voice small. "Isn't a whole hallmark of b-being in love not really making sense but going with the emotions if they're too big? Isn't that all a part of the excitement?"

"Sure it is," Declan says. "That's kind of Cupid's whole business model."

"Cupid might not even be a real person," Luca retorts. "But you know who's been a real person this whole time?" He presses a hand to his fuchsia bow tie. "I have. I've stood by your side for years. I have seen you through the worst and best. I *kissed* you and you didn't—"

"I said I wanted to forget that," I murmur. "Luca, I *don't* like you in that way. I—I told you—"

"C'mon, Joy. You're asexual." Luca spits out the word as if he'd just drank poison accidentally. "What do you even know about romance?"

His words send a river of ice coursing through my body, tightening all my muscles.

"When I came out, you supported me," I say quietly, so as not to make a scene. "Was that all just an act? Were you just playing the good guy? Was Christmas Eve all part of your plan? Did you ever actually care? Or was this whole thing some long-winded way of making me feel obligated to love you? Oh wait, I can't know what love is, right?"

Anxiety brews in my stomach, as I rethink every single interaction Luca and I have had throughout our senior year alone.

"Luca," Valentina hisses. "What the fuck?"

"Val," Luca says, "you're—"

"What is wrong with you?" Yasmine says. "You're supposed to be Joy's friend. Not some jealous tool."

"Jealous?" Luca repeats, incredulous. "How am I—"

"Have you been an acephobic asshole all along?" My spine is becoming steel, whether because of the way that all this stress is making every sound press on my ears or the muscle spasms coursing through my body, I have no idea. "Or did you become one after I didn't kiss you back?"

"You don't know what you want," Luca continues as if I hadn't said anything. "Val does. You, Joy, love *scares* you. Doesn't—"

"Shut up!" I close my eyes and cram my hands over my ears, blocking out the sounds around us. Blaring pop music, conversations, laughter, sweet nothings whispered on the gentle lap of

the lake all dampen against my sweaty palms. I sink into the muffling, even as the fingers on my left hand scratch the side of my face, just below my earlobe. The tiny cut stings, same as the hot tears welling up in my eyes and clouding my glasses as I squat in my dress. "Just shut up, Luca! Please!"

My voice cracks through my ears.

"Joy." Valentina crouches beside me. "C'mon," she soothes. "It's okay. Do you want us to . . . ?" Her words trail off and I shake my head.

"No," I whisper through the wetness in my throat. "You two go dance, please. D-Don't worry about me."

"Don't be silly," Val starts. But I cut her off.

"Seriously, please. This is important to you both, so it's important to me."

I exhale a breath that's somehow both tight and shaky at once. Stumbling to my feet, I pry my hands from my ears and blink Central Park back into view. The fairy lights dance across my vision. The music rushes through my head as I shake it.

Luca is gone.

He's walking into the crowd behind Vikram and Declan, who are adjusting their blazers as though they just tossed him out of the prom.

"We can take you home if you want," Yasmine says. "Seriously, if you want to turn this night into watching nature documentaries on Netflix in our prom dresses as we eat ice cream, we can."

"No." My heart swells as I look at her and Valentina. "I-I'll be okay. I just . . ." I sigh, wiping at my damp eyelashes under my glasses. "You go have fun."

"Are you sure?" Valentina asks softly.

"Yes." I nod, sniffling. "I'm sure."

After hugging both Yasmine and Valentina, I watch as they head to the dance floor and immediately become wrapped up in each other's arms. Declan and Eitan follow them, and Vikram goes to join his castmates from *Pippin* as they immediately begin a rendition of "Magic to Do," singing over the top of the music.

They all go off to dance, and suddenly it's just Nathaniel and me, standing across from each other.

"Here," Nathaniel says instead. "Let's go somewhere quieter." He pulls a pair of purple earplugs from the breast pocket of his button-down. "You can take these." My mouth flutters open as I try to formulate a response. "I experience sound sensitivity, too," he explains. "Sometimes, this city is too loud. But you need these more than I do at the moment. Come with me."

After I slip the earplugs in, we walk toward Bethesda Terrace. Passing by the stairs leading to the upper level, we step into the shadows of the terrace itself, dipping underneath one of the archways.

Once my back touches the textured wall, I take the earplugs out and offer them back to Nathaniel. "Thank you," I murmur.

"You're welcome." Nathaniel's voice is gentle in the darkness, same as the sandstone against my shoulders. "Joy, I . . ." He sighs. ". . . I need to tell you something."

I look up at him, shivering from wind passing across my shoulders.

"I . . ." Nathaniel's breast pocket rustles as he puts his earplugs away. "I'm sorry for how Luca treated you just now. I . . ." His voice trails off. ". . . I wish I had advice to offer you, tell you how to navigate this."

"Oh, it's fine." I shake my head even though he can't see it. "You don't need to do that."

"But we're a community," he explains. "Joy, I'm queer, too. I'm pan. I feel like I need to be here for you."

For the first time since falling off his coffee table, my heart flutters at Nathaniel's words.

"Well, you got me away from all the noise," I say. "So, you did help. Thank you, for that and for . . . sharing a bit of yourself with me."

"Tell you what." Nathaniel clears his throat. "Would you like to get out of here?"

I check my phone again. It's 6:03. I gaze back toward the group of students dancing and laughing. Is Cupid out there waiting for me?

They'd understand me needing to leave prom early; I know they would.

"Where would we go?" I ask.

“The Dog and Moon?” Nathaniel suggests. “My brother is supposed to get engaged there tonight, and I don’t want to miss it.”

“That is so romantic.” I smile. “I will come, but only if I get to sing Irish folk songs.”

“You know Irish folk songs?” Nathaniel asks as we leave the terrace and walk up the stairs, me clinging to the railing and him walking beside me.

“Yeah.” I nod. “I’m Irish American, both from my momma and whoever my sperm donor dad is.” I pause. “But I’m not the best singer.”

“Joy,” Nathaniel murmurs as we continue up the rest of the stairs. “Somehow, I doubt that.”

My cheeks flush at his belief in me. “I just need to send a quick email before we go.”

To: Caldwell Cupid (cupid@caldwellcupid.com)

From: Joy Corvi (joy.corvi@caldwell.edu)

Date: May 16, 6:05 p.m.

Subject: RE: RE: RE: A Promposal

Dear Cupid,

You will not believe the night I have had. I am so sorry to have to do this, but let's reschedule. I will explain everything.

Yours,

Joy

CHAPTER TWENTY-EIGHT

NATHANIEL

Joy is in love with Cupid.

Joy is in love with Cupid.

Joy is in love with Cupid.

Those words repeat in my head the entire ride on the C train to Hell's Kitchen, through the short walk to the Dog and Moon, as my phone buzzes in my pocket. But when we step inside the pub, the music is too loud for my existential crisis.

Franny immediately pulls me to the side. "Hey!" She sweeps me into a hug. "Oh, I'm so glad you're here to see this!" she whispers gleefully. "Joy, hi!" She hugs Joy next, who smiles back at her. "Here, let me introduce you. This is my brother Warren, his wife, Belinda, and my boyfriend, Daniel."

"It's nice to see you again," Joy says. "And it's nice to meet everyone." Her voice sounds so happy that my body relaxes. My shoulders have been stiff all day, tight with anticipation for how the night was supposed to go. I was supposed to get to the Bethesda Terrace when my friends made their way to the dance floor. I was going to wait right outside its arches. I planned to turn to Joy, take a deep breath, and say the words I know she deserves to hear.

"Joy, I'm Caldwell Cupid."

But Luca ruined everything.

I know I could have told Joy when we were standing there in the dark together. But the moment wasn't right. She was sad and confused. The night was too full of the hateful things Luca said.

"And that," a guy with an impressive brown beard and a banjo in his arms says from behind the mic stand, "was 'Here's a Health to the Company.'" He smiles. "One of my favorites I do, at faire or anywhere. As always, I'm Andrew McDermott, and thank you for joining us tonight. The rest of the guys will be back in a second, but . . ." He nods out into the audience. "There is someone here who needs this stage more than I do." He winks, walking down the ramp off to the side.

Arthur wheels up onto the stage, situating his chair beneath the warm glow of the lights hung above it. "Everett," he says, looking off to the side. "I need you up here, please."

My brother joins him on the stage, his hands in the pockets

of his dark blue jeans. "Are you going to serenade me?" he asks, curious.

"Not exactly," Arthur chuckles. "I can't sing." He reaches into the breast pocket of his deep red button-down and pulls out a ring box, holding it in his palm.

"Arthur," Everett whispers, his voice breathless. He puts his hand over his mouth, his shoulders lurching. "Oh God. Babe, are you . . . are you serious?"

"Very much so," Arthur murmurs. He sniffs back tears as he opens the box.

"Yes," Everett says immediately.

"Wait." Arthur gazes up at him, his eyes gleaming. "I need to actually ask you the question first." That earns a few chuckles from the crowd and Everett himself. "Now." He clears his throat, squaring his shoulders. "Everett Gabriel Wright, I love you. And I want to spend the rest of my life with you. Will you be my husband?"

"Oh, Arthur, I love you, too." Everett sinks to his knees, shaking with tears. Happy ones from how big his smile is as he whispers, "And yes. Yes, I will."

The entire pub erupts into cheers as Arthur slips the ring on my brother's finger and they kiss. My brother and his new fiancé get swallowed up by the rest of the audience, Everett in Arthur's lap as Arthur moves his wheelchair.

The band makes their way back up to the stage and launches into a song.

"Hey." Joy nudges my shoulder. "Let's dance. Neither of us got to at prom."

"You want to dance?" I ask, raising my eyebrows at her as she grins. "With me?"

"Sure," she says. "What did I get all dressed up for?"

"Fair point." I grin back at her as she takes both of my hands in hers. We fall into the lyrics of "The Rocky Road to Dublin," same as I fall into our words when we write them to each other.

But just for tonight I let those thoughts fall away.

All I can think about right now is this beautiful girl I'm dancing with, her arms now looped around my neck, my hands resting on her hips as we sway. Both of us singing the song at the top of our lungs. Neither of us can sing it on key, but I'm having too much fun to care, for what is perhaps the first time in my life.

Once Andrew brings the song to a close, Joy and I stop dancing, leaning against each other for support. I exhale the kind of warm, ragged breaths that usually mean my inhaler should be at the ready. And Joy rests her head on my chest.

"That," she murmurs, her left hand tangling with my fingers, "was amazing."

"Yeah," I murmur back. "It was." I take a few puffs of my inhaler, not realizing that I have tears rolling down my cheeks until after the second dose.

I'm unsure when I started crying, but I wipe my face with the back of my hand.

Because I don't know how much longer I'll have Joy in my life once I tell her what I meant to tonight. And I want to keep these feelings about her as close as I possibly can.

To: Caldwell Cupid (cupid@caldwellcupid.com)

From: Luca Sapienti (luca.sapienti@caldwell.edu)

Date: May 16, 10:00 p.m.

Subject: (No Subject)

I've tried writing to you about Joy for months, and you haven't helped me.

And now she's in love with you?

For fuck's sake, I knew she'd been writing to you, but falling for you? What the hell? Do you feel the same about her?

You know she's ace, right?

To: Luca Sapienti (luca.sapienti@caldwell.edu)

From: Caldwell Cupid (cupid@caldwellcupid.com)

Date: May 16, 11:00 p.m.

Subject: RE: (No Subject)

Luca,

I have not been responding to you because I cannot make someone fall in love with you.

You may have known Joy for years, but you clearly don't respect her. You don't respect her kindness, her beauty, or her queerness. At all. You only see her as the person you want instead of the person she is.

I will not help you.

Cupid

To: Caldwell Cupid (cupid@caldwellcupid.com)

From: Joy Corvi (joy.corvi@caldwell.edu)

Date: May 16, 11:10 p.m.

Subject: RE: RE: RE: A Promposal

Dear Cupid,

I'm sorry about prom night. Can we meet at graduation instead?

Yours,

Joy

(Mail returned to sender. Email address no longer valid.)

CHAPTER TWENTY-NINE

NATHANIEL

On Sunday, I'm woken up by both the patter of raindrops on my window and someone knocking on my bedroom door.

I yawn as I sit up in bed, my covers falling down past my hips.

"Nathaniel?" Mother asks from the hallway. "Your father and I need you in the living room."

"I'll be down in a minute," I say.

After pulling on a pair of jeans, a plain green polo, and a pair of argyle socks, I pad downstairs. But when I walk into the living room, my heart falls out of my body and slides onto the hardwood floors.

On the coffee table is a pile of emails Caldwell Cupid sent to Joy. A pile of emails *I* wrote to Joy. Months and months of secrets and hopes composed when the rest of the city was asleep.

Now, our words are in my living room.

"I . . ." The single letter is a shard of glass that cuts the inside of my throat. I expect blood to gather somewhere around my vocal cords, but bile just rises instead. "I can explain."

"Oh," Father huffs from the couch. His mustache twitches as he gestures at the letters. "We certainly hope you can, Nathaniel. You're pansexual? So, in addition to being utterly confused about your future, you're also confused about your sexuality?"

"No, no," I croak. "I'm not confused. I know what I am." I swallow hard as my throat constricts. "How did . . ." I blink at them, hoping they'll somehow disappear. "Where did they come from?"

"They were on our stoop this morning," Mother explains coldly from her place next to him. "Not even in our mailbox. Just sitting out there in the open. Anyone could have found them and read them." She plucks a piece of loose-leaf notebook paper from the end table; I can only briefly glimpse at the neat, blocky handwriting. "There was this note explaining that you are someone called Caldwell Cupid." Fear grips my stomach, but she continues, oblivious. "We've read all of them. Who is Joy? Why does she know about your *confusion* before we do?"

"I'm not confused," I plead instead, despising how weak my voice is. "I'm not. I know exactly who I am. And I'm not sorry I didn't talk to you about this before. You've never been open to these kinds of conversations."

"Well, you know our views on all of that," Father says. He

waves his hand as if that could brush my queerness away. "People can do what they want, and we'll treat any kind of patient who comes to us, but we don't allow that in our family. It's not what God wants."

I try to push back the pain in my throat, but it courses through the rest of my body, weighing down my lungs, bones, and muscles. "Since when do you care about what God thinks?" Air hisses through my lungs. "Do you two even pray anymore?"

"We prayed every day that your mother was pregnant with you," Father points out, his voice tight. "She prayed that she could carry you to term." At his words, Mother bursts into tears, burying her face in her hands. But Father doesn't reach for her; he stays focused on me instead. "And this is how you repay God's grace to our family?" he asks me. "By being queer?"

"Father," I splutter. "Listen to me. Please—"

"Nathaniel." Mother rises to her feet. Her face is pink, her eyes glossy from her sobs. "If this is how you want to live your life, your father and I agreed that you are no longer welcome in this house. Or this family."

"We need you to leave," Father continues, putting his arm around Mother.

My stomach now joins my heart on the floor as bile continues to churn up my throat. I put my hand over my mouth to keep from throwing up, lurching forward.

"Where am I supposed to go?" I whisper to the bay window as thunder rumbles beyond its panes.

"That doesn't concern us," Father tells me. "You no longer concern us. Leave now, Nathaniel."

The only thing I take before I leave both my parents behind are my sneakers from the hallway closet.

I end up at Everett's apartment building shivering in the lobby, my chest heaving from an asthma attack. I press the button for his unit, leaning against the intercom panel, trying to take deep breaths and calm down.

But when Everett's voice fills the tiny room, my asthma attack only gets worse.

"Hello?" he answers.

"Everett," I wheeze. "I—I need help."

"Stay there," he tells me. "I'm coming down."

Everett meets me in the lobby, looking more casual than I've ever seen him in an old pair of jeans and an NYU School of Medicine T-shirt. "What's wrong?" he asks gently.

I wheeze, shaking my head, unable to speak from how much my chest hurts.

"Easy," my brother soothes. He takes my wrist in his hand, nodding to himself a moment later. "One hundred and twelve beats per minute. Do you have your inhaler?"

"No." The word is little more than a hiss of air.

"I need you to stand up straight for me." Everett carefully

pulls me away from the wall, helping me stand with my spine flush against it instead. "Take slow, deep breaths. Here, I'll do them with you."

After breathing together for a few minutes, I calm a bit. Everett nods. "Good, good. Come up to the apartment with me, and we can talk, okay?"

"Okay," I whisper. Now that my asthma attack has dissipated, all the emotions from earlier flood my body instead, and I am grateful that Everett doesn't feel the need to talk during the elevator ride.

But the moment we enter his unit—a decent-sized place with white walls, colorful canvas prints of the city, big windows, gleaming hardwood, and a gray sectional in the living room—I finally burst into tears.

"Nathaniel." My brother wraps his arms around me, and I collapse against his shoulder. "What happened?"

"Mother and Father," I sob. "Th-They found out I'm pansexual, and they kicked me out of the house. And—And they weren't going to pay for me to attend CIB before all of this, so now I don't really have a future, do I?"

"Oh God," Everett whispers. "I'm so sorry." He swallows, his voice tight with his own tears. "Okay, first of all, you're safe here."

"We promise," Arthur says from nearby. "I'll get my office cleared out, and we'll ask our friends if anyone has a bed they aren't using."

"You'll always have a home here," my brother tells me. "As long as it's all right with my fiancé."

"Of course," Arthur replies.

"Really?" I murmur, leaning against the door as I look at them. "Are you sure?"

"Nathaniel, I'm marrying your brother," Arthur says. "We'll be family soon, so our home is yours."

"Thank you," I murmur.

"You can sleep on the sectional for now," Everett continues. "I'll get you a change of clothes. I'll call Franny and Warren, too. They're going to want to know what happened, and you need to have your things. We can both take the day off tomorrow, so—"

"No." I shake my head.

"It's okay to take a day off," Arthur says. "You'll need time to readjust to your new normal."

"School is my normalcy," I murmur. "It's one of the only normal things I have left. I need to go. Please."

Everett and Arthur look at each other, both of their eyes filled with a kind of deep sadness that I'm only just beginning to experience.

"Who am I to tell the valedictorian he can't go to school?" Everett sighs. "Speaking of." He clears his throat. "I don't want you worrying about college. Between your siblings' salaries, we can make it work."

I stare at him, wiping tears from my face with both

hands. "Are you serious?" I manage to ask, sniffing.

"Yes." Everett nods, resolute. "Nathaniel, you're going to be a gifted ob-gyn someday, and I'm not letting our parents ruin that for you."

"Thank you," I murmur again.

Later that night, both Franny and Warren burst through the apartment door, squabbling over who gets to hug me first. Franny wins by ducking underneath our brother's massive arm. She drops the cardboard box she's carrying and pulls me to her.

"Nathaniel!" Franny squeezes my shoulders when we part, craning her neck to look up at me. "Are you okay?" She looks at Arthur and Everett, who are lounging on their sectional, with Everett's head in his fiancé's lap. "Can you believe our parents?" she hisses. "For God's sake. I swear, *I'm* about to propose to Daniel myself just so I can change my last name."

"I'm already talking to Belinda about changing mine," Warren replies, giving me a fierce hug after Franny lets go. "What do you think about Warren Bearden?"

"Solid choice." I crouch down to the box on the floor. I dig through it to find my inhaler, my phone, and my charger. My heart warms when I realize that Franny brought a few of my romance books.

"Where's Natalie?" Everett asks as I plug in my phone. "Did you leave her with our parents?"

"No." Franny scoffs. "Absolutely not. I don't want their queerphobic bullshit around my baby. She's at Daniel's." She sighs. "I move into my own apartment next week, so we're staying with him for now."

"Huh," Warren muses. "I knew I was right to introduce you."

"Well, *I* introduced you to Belinda." Franny playfully shoves his arm, her eyes bright when she looks at Everett. "Do you have anything to drink?"

Arthur tells her where the cider is in the fridge, and as everyone else cracks open bottles, I feel as if my heartbeat finally returns to a normal pace.

It turns out it's nearly impossible to sleep on a sectional when you're six-four.

As I'm readjusting my shoulders against the couch and pulling my blanket farther up my chest, I hear the low rumble of voices from down the hallway, mixing with the late-night noise of Union Square below. I know I should just close my eyes, but I stand up instead. Walking slowly over to the doorway, I wince as the wooden floor creaks underneath my bare feet.

". . . I don't give a fuck what time it is," Everett hisses. "So, I'm asking again: What kind of parents throw out their son? Did you even consider the psychological effects this will have on Nathaniel? You don't *agree* with—" He pauses, taking a deep breath. "You don't just have one queer son, you know."

My stomach tightens at his words, and I draw my arms around it, the blanket becoming taut against my shoulders.

"I'm gay." The sentence breaks apart in my brother's mouth. "And I never told you because I *knew* that you'd react like this." His voice fades into tears. "You would have kicked me out, just like you did Nathaniel this morning. I would've had nowhere to go. But Nathaniel came here because he *knew* my fiancé and I would keep him safe.

"Yes, I'm engaged," Everett continues. "And he loves me more than either of you are capable of.

"No, I didn't do it for him. I transferred because I was worried that the surgeons at St. Thomas's would realize I was gay and would tell you before I could." He pauses again. "You should be ashamed of the people you are, and what you have done."

Everett ends the call, and I hear him lean against the wall. He starts to sob, big, gasping breaths that mingle with Arthur's voice.

"Everett," he murmurs. "You didn't have to call them."

"I wanted to," Everett replies, sniffling. "Arthur, my brother didn't deserve any of this. He's such a good kid."

"I know, I know," Arthur soothes.

Tears run down my cheeks as I take a step backward. The floor creaks under my foot again, and I grit my teeth against the noise.

"Nathaniel?" my brother calls, his voice wet. "What are you doing up?"

I bite back a curse and step into the darkened hallway. Even with just the light trickling from Everett and Arthur's bedroom, I see a framed photograph of them at Pride hung on the wall. They're kissing in a sea of rainbows, their love for each other written all over their faces.

How could our parents have a problem with that?

"I . . . I'm sorry." A fresh batch of hot tears wells up in my eyes as I walk toward Everett. "You—" Before I finish that sentence, we throw our arms around each other.

I break against Everett's shoulder, and he collapses into mine.

"Nathaniel," my brother says between his own sobs. "I need you to listen to me, okay?"

"Okay," I whisper.

"You're safe here," Everett promises. "You always will be. Arthur and I promise you that. Now." He draws away from me, clearing his throat and squaring his shoulders. "I think we all should try and get some rest."

He and Arthur head to their bedroom, and I stumble back to the sectional. Wiping my eyes, I wait until I hear the click of their door before I grab my phone.

I navigate to the email app I use for Caldwell Cupid, more out of a need for normalcy than anything else. I can't exactly tell Joy about what happened today, but I can at least write to her. Apologize for Cupid not showing up at prom. Tell her we can meet at graduation instead.

But when I click on it, a white screen with black text greets me: This domain is no longer active.

In all the commotion I hadn't had time to wonder about who set this all in motion. A chill courses through my body. I lean against the sectional, the words boring into my eyes as a realization makes my stomach sink.

Someone hacked my Caldwell Cupid account.

That's how my parents read the copies of my emails.

There is only one person in all of Caldwell Preparatory Academy who's skilled enough with computers to do that. And he just happens to be pissed at me.

CHAPTER THIRTY

JOY

I'm barely listening to Val and Yasmine chatting as we walk into the school building. I can't stop staring at the bold notification on my screen. Why would they do this? Was this all just a joke? Now I might never know who I was telling all my deepest feelings to.

When we walk through the glass doors of our academy, my heart freezes. Its chill spreads from my ribs to the rest of my body, contorting my arms and legs into muscle spasms, rooting me to the tile floor.

Papers are taped to the walls.

Not just papers.

Printouts of emails.

The emails Caldwell Cupid wrote to me.

And the emails I wrote to them.

All my thoughts and fears and longings and confessions of love.

Wallpapered around the academy for everyone to read.

And there on the bulletin board in the center of the room someone has written in black marker: NATHANIEL WRIGHT IS CALDWELL CUPID.

My friends may say my name, but I don't hear them. Instead, I lurch forward, my legs screaming at me until I reach the bulletin board. Grabbing as many letters as will fit in my arms, I pivot painfully on my left heel and push through the throngs of students who are standing around reading.

"I need to find him," I whisper to the paper and ink in my hands. To the promises and sweet words he wrote to me.

Before I can think of where to go, Nathaniel collides with me. His arms are also full of letters. His face is as pale as milk. His blue eyes gaze down into mine, filled with every single emotion we've written to each other about over the last five months.

The confusion. The desire. The fear. The longing.

The love.

"I-It's you." I stumble to my feet. "You're Caldwell Cupid."

"Joy," Nathaniel whispers, swallowing hard. "I can explain."

"Y-You were writing to me," I hiss. My muscles tighten, and I use their spasming to keep the tears inside, despite them desperately wanting to spill down my cheeks. "Was this entire thing some elaborate plan to throw me off?"

"No." Nathaniel drops his letters, holding out his hands.

"Joy, no. Please, can we talk about this later? Somewhere else?" He glances around, and I follow him. A sizable group of students has gathered around us, whispering.

"Meet me at my brother's apartment," Nathaniel says. "After school. I . . . I live there now." He swallows hard again. "Just let me explain and then if you want, you never have to see or speak to me again."

A white-hot fury blooms in my chest, but there is something like sadness in Nathaniel's eyes that dulls my anger. "Fine, I'll come," I murmur, my chest tight. "But I promise, that will be the last time either of us says a word to the other." Gesturing to the letters scattered around our feet, I add, "We've already said so much."

"I know." Nathaniel's voice has shrunk. "I know we have. But you deserve to know more. You deserve the whole truth. I'll text you the address."

The bell rings and the students leave for class. Nathaniel turns around, headed for the hallway where his locker is. But I stay in the lobby, unable to bring myself to move.

"Joy," Valentina says. "C'mon. Class will help you get your mind off . . . this."

"She's right," Yasmine adds. "Let's go."

"Well?" Luca suddenly emerges from the same hallway Nathaniel just went down.

I stare at him. We haven't spoken since the fiasco at prom over the weekend and I was fine with that.

“Wh-What?” I ask, glaring at him. “You want to gloat about how you were right or—”

“How does it feel?” Luca interjects. “Knowing that you’ve fallen in love with”—he gasps, his hand over the Caldwell Preparatory Academy emblem on his blazer, mocking me—“your rival?”

“Luca,” Valentina says. “Knock it off. She doesn’t need you making it worse.”

“All you do is make things worse,” Yasmine adds. “You’ve been this way since New Year’s. All she did was decide to go away to school. It isn’t the end of the world.”

“It was to me,” Luca snaps. “You two have each other. Joy and I were supposed to have each other, too.”

“Listen.” I glare at him. “Just because we’ve known each other for most of our lives doesn’t mean that you’re entitled to me.”

“Believe me.” Luca folds his arms across his chest. “It would’ve been so simple. But you had to actually go and ruin it with Cupid.” He snorts. “When you told us you were in love with them, I knew I had to see who they were. So, I hacked into the website after prom.”

“Y-You did this?” I whisper.

“Do you realize how fucked up that is?” Valentina demands.

“Joy is her own person,” Yasmine tells Luca. “She gets to decide what her love life looks like.”

"*I'm* the one Joy should be with," Luca says, turning to me. "You hate Nate. I knew that once you found out he was the one behind all these letters you would come to your senses."

"Don't pretend you did this for me," I say, willing my voice not to shake. "It was for *you*. All of this. You thought you could *make* me love you."

"Please, Joy. You've been my best friend, forever. It's meant to be, it's perfect," he mutters. "You should stay here and be with me. Don't go to CIB just to fill some diversity quota."

My mouth falls open. The blood that had frozen over when I stepped into school has thawed, fire now coursing through my veins instead. "Excuse me?" I hiss. *"A diversity quota?"*

"Well, yeah." Luca shrugs, adjusting his glasses. "Colleges like to have some disabled students, don't they?"

"You think *that's* why I got accepted? I couldn't get accepted into one of the top choice science colleges in the country on my own?" I demand. "What do you think all my work these past four years was actually for?" I shake my head. "You know what? I don't need an answer for that. This whole time, you've been so worried we would drift apart when I move to California, but you've just sped along the timeline. Our friendship is *over*, Luca." I bend down to gather the letters at my feet. "I need to clean these up." Valentina and Yasmine step in between me and Luca until he gives up and walks away.

My friends and I begin to peel the emails off the walls and

from the bulletin board. "So," Valentina says, dumping a pile of emails into the nearby garbage can. "You're really going to talk to Nathaniel after school?"

"Yeah." I pluck the last email from the bulletin board, crumpling it up before throwing it away. "I am. I—I need to hear what he has to say."

CHAPTER THIRTY-ONE

JOY

I can't quiet the questions spinning around in my head. *If this wasn't some plan to throw me off, then what was it? Did I actually mean anything to Nathaniel at all? Because he has grown to mean something to me—*

I run my spidery left fingers along my dress as I knock on the door with my right hand. The soft fabric calms me, but my body spasms as Nathaniel pulls the door open.

"Joy—" he begins.

"Was all of this just a joke?" I ask, walking inside.

"A joke?" Nathaniel repeats incredulously, his blue eyes wide. He closes the door behind us. Our hands flutter to our ears as it slams shut. The sound pounds against my eardrums, only making my confusion that much more disorienting. "What do you mean 'a joke'?"

I fold my arms over my chest, watching it swell over the

neckline of my dress as I breathe. "The 'let the disabled girl thinks she has actually found someone who loves her' joke."

"Excuse me?" Nathaniel's mouth falls open; his voice creaks around in his throat. "How could you think I would do something like that?"

"If I wasn't a joke, then was I a project?" I ask, leaning against the door. "When I first wrote to you, did you think that you'd be able to teach an ace girl about romance?" Tears prick my eyes. "Because it's not like I-I'd understand that, right?"

Memories from what Luca said at prom pound against my skull. I clench my left hand, hoping the pain from my fingernails digging into my palm will keep me from crying.

"No," he whispers. "I . . . You have to know that I *never* thought of you like that. All those emails. All those . . . love letters." His voice trembles on the last two words. "They were true. They are how I feel. What I think of you."

"How am I supposed to believe that now?" My stomach flips at the reality that Nathaniel Wright actually has feelings for me, and that I've been cultivating my own for him. "When you never told me who you are?"

"I wanted to," he says. A few blond curls splay against his forehead. "So many times."

"Why didn't you?" I ask. "You had *five months* t-to tell me!"

"I was scared!" As Nathaniel shouts those words, his shoulders drop, and he crumples in on himself. "And it's not like I communicate well outside of writing letters, so I didn't know how to tell you. I know that doesn't make up for what I did. I know it doesn't fix lying to you for all this. I am *so* sorry."

"You were scared?" I interject. My hands come undone, my left one staying level with my breast. "Why would someone like you have any reason to be scared about . . . love, romance, any of that?"

He blinks. "What do you mean?"

"Nathaniel, look at you." I stare up at him. At this boy with blue eyes, gold curls, and a face so beautiful that the sun itself would be jealous. "You're so smart that you're the valedictorian and bound for medical school. You're so *attractive* . . ." My cheeks flush at the word. But I'm past the point of denying that I find him as such. ". . . that you could be a model if you wanted."

"You think I'm attractive?" Nathaniel asks in a small voice. He moves closer, gazing down into my eyes. "Because, Joy, I . . . I think you're beautiful."

Beautiful.

The word sends a warmth pulsing throughout my entire body. I've never been called beautiful this way, much less imagined someone would ever think of me in that context.

I can't quite let myself believe it.

"Be realistic," I whisper. My eyes break from his, roving over my own body. A body I love, but that the rest of the world looks at as less than. "I'm beautiful to you?"

"Yes." Slowly, Nathaniel reaches for my left hand. I extend it to him, and soon, our fingers are woven together. Mine spasm between his, which only makes me move close enough to him to have our chests touch.

"What do you see that others don't?" I blink up at him. "Tell me."

Nathaniel bends down so that his forehead brushes mine. "Joy." My name is little more than breath across my mouth. "I see the girl I have been in love with for four years."

"S-So." The word trembles on its way out of my mouth. "You think I'm beautiful? And you *love* me?"

"Yes," Nathaniel whispers. "I *love* you, Joy." He pauses as those four words float in what little air there is between us. "Please, don't feel obligated to say it back."

"I will," I murmur, already knowing the truth. "In my own time. But for now . . . can you kiss me?"

"Of course." Nathaniel's hands brace my hips as my right hand comes to rest on his shoulder. "Wait." Our noses brush as the heat of his mouth caresses mine. "What are you, um—"

"Comfortable with?" I finish, my voice no more than a whisper. He nods, his curls falling against my bangs as I think. "Well," I begin, "I'm comfortable with kissing. And you can touch me."

"You can touch me, too," he whispers.

Then, Nathaniel lifts me up into his arms. I wrap my legs around his waist, my soft body resting against his, made of defined muscles. And when Nathaniel finally press his lips to mine, he crushes both of us to the apartment door.

My hands find the hem of his polo—which I now realize is the same shade of pink as my dress—and together, we yank it over his head. It falls to the floor, and I pull away from him, just slightly. His hands finds my hips again, mine come back to resting on his shoulders, just as they had the night we danced at the Dog and Moon.

As my hands travel along his chest, Nathaniel carries us past the entryway and into the living room. He lays me across a sectional, both of us bouncing on the plush softness. His hands begin to rove down my body, each new part he touches blossoming with warmth. His lips leave mine, trailing along my cheek, down my jaw, and coming to rest at the base of my throat.

"Joy." Practically sighed against my skin, Nathaniel embraces my name with so much love, so much . . . *longing* that tears well up in my eyes. "I—" He pauses. "Are you crying? I'm sorry, I didn't mean to—"

"No," I murmur, closing my eyes as the pads of his thumbs brush away the wetness off my cheeks. "I'm not sad. I'm just . . . so happy."

"Oh." Nathaniel laughs gently. The word hitches on his own small cry. "I am, too." He rolls his body off mine, but we pull each other close again. His hair is tousled, his cheeks are as pink as our clothes, and his lips are swollen from our kissing.

From how his hand touches my cheek again, from the light in his eyes, I'm thinking I look about the same.

"Um." The word teeters on Nathaniel's tongue as he smiles the tiniest bit. "Will you be my girlfriend?"

"Yes." I kiss him again, both of us cradling the other's face in our hands when we stop. "Will you be my boyfriend?"

"Yes." He kisses me back, and the way both of us are smiling when we break apart fills my heart with more love than I thought it was possible for it to hold.

CHAPTER THIRTY-TWO

NATHANIEL

Over the next month, I kiss Joy whenever the opportunity presents itself.

In my room, in her room, in the subway, everywhere.

We both figured we had to make up for the four years where we were arguing.

When I told Joy about coming out to my parents and them kicking me out, she held me as I cried, promising to be there for me if I needed anyone. I've been lucky enough to have support from my girlfriend, our friends, and my siblings. Along with weekly sessions at the Rainbow Center with my counselor, Jen, I've started to adjust to my new normal.

And it feels nice, even as Franny chastises me while lugging a cardboard box into my room the evening before the last day of school.

"I love you," she huffs, perching herself on my bed. It's a

twin, made comfortable by a CIB bedspread Arthur and Everett surprised me with. "But who the hell organizes every assignment they've ever done?"

"It's called being meticulous. I've done it for years." I withdraw a purple binder from the box. I color-code my classes, so this one is weighty with AP English assignments. "That's a hallmark of a good doctor, right?"

Franny blows a strand of blond hair out of her face. "Well, sure," she says. "I guess you're right." She gets to her feet. "That was the last box from your old room."

"Did you"—I pull at the collar of my blue-and-white striped polo—"see them at all?"

"Nope." Franny shakes her head, not needing to ask who I mean. "They're probably working, as usual. I'm lucky they forgot to make sure I don't have a key to the place anymore." She stretches her arms above her head, the puffy sleeves of her beige blouse falling back a little bit. "I just came by to drop this off. Warren is watching Natalie, and I have a date with Daniel, so I need to get ready." She sweeps me into a hug. "Love you."

"Love you, too," I say when she lets go. "Thanks for this."

"You're welcome." Franny smiles at me before leaving just as quickly as she arrived, and I settle into the quiet.

Union Square bustles below me, sounds that have become as familiar as my room. But inside, the only noises are my socked feet on the wooden floor and laminated papers rustling as I double-check their order.

When I get to my AP Biology binder—a bright green one—however, my fingers freeze on a paper from last December. My paper on cellular structure.

It's the only paper I received a 99 percent on all year. The paper Joy and I argued about in the hallway the day before the holiday break.

"I'm not valedictorian," I whisper, the words making my stomach whoosh. The pads of my fingers skate across the laminate sheet, as though I can feel the raised printed ink through them. "Joy is."

Throwing the binder back into the box Franny had brought me, I dive at the desk beneath my bedroom window that overlooks Union Square Park, powering up my laptop.

I have to write a letter.

To: Michelle Mason (michelle.mason@caldwell.edu)

From: Nathaniel Wright (nathaniel.wright@caldwell.edu)

Date: June 18, 7:07 p.m.

Subject: Incorrect Valedictorian

Dear Principal Mason,

I have reason to believe that I am not the rightful valedictorian of this year's senior class at Caldwell Preparatory Academy. I will be coming by your office first thing in the morning to discuss this with you.

Sincerely,

Nathaniel Wright

CHAPTER THIRTY-THREE

JOY

"He'll be here soon," Valentina says from my dining table. "Your lips deserve this break, anyway."

It's graduation morning, and we are wearing our purple graduation robes and rainbow honors cords. Valentina's holding her mortarboard in her hands, tilting it in the light. "Do you think it needs more glitter?" she asks us.

"It looks great." Yasmine kisses her. "Perfect, actually."

Valentina grins, kissing her back. "Thanks."

"And *my* lips need a break?" I joke.

Val had decorated her cap with a galaxy, specifically using both the colors of the lesbian and asexual pride flags. Yasmine had her cheerleading squad sign hers around the logo for NYIT. Mine has a copy of a photo featuring me and Ma. She was wearing blue scrubs, bouncing me on her hip as I had a play stethoscope around my neck. I created a border of the pride flag around it, too.

When I showed the completed cap to my moms, we all cried. And then Ma presented me with a blanket featuring both the ace and pan pride colors. Momma said she'd started knitting it the same night I told them. That made me cry harder.

The intercom buzzes and I run over to it, holding my robe up so that I don't trip over my feet. "Hello?" I ask, bouncing with anticipation.

"Joy?" I can already hear the smile in Nathaniel's voice. "It's me."

I leave the door open so that he can let himself in when he gets upstairs. "Happy graduation day!" he shouts, walking through the door and kissing me just above the bridge of my glasses.

"Happy graduation day," I reply, kissing him back.

"I have something for you," he says. "Come here."

Without a word, he takes off his valedictorian regalia and slips it over my head.

"That's sweet." I laugh. "But that's not how this works. You earned this."

"Actually, I didn't." Nathaniel raises his eyebrows and smirks like he has a secret. "We've been neck and neck on most of our tests and papers, except for one," he explains.

"The paper on cellular structure," I whisper, remembering.

"Exactly." He smiles. "You did better than me by one whole percent. So, I went to Principal Mason a few days ago, and we went through everything together. It was just finalized last night. I brought proof, in case you didn't believe me." He hands me a stack of thick black binders. "I organize my assignments, so I just consolidated these for you. It's every assignment we've had this year."

My mouth falls open, my stomach dips, and I kiss Nathaniel until I need to actually use my lungs to breathe.

"What?!" Valentina and Yasmine shriek.

"So, the administration just made some kind of mistake?" Valentina says, eyes wide. "That's a pretty big mistake!"

"Well, I don't think it was a mistake," Nathaniel almost whispers.

"Luca." All four of us say in unison as I head toward the door.

Wrenching it open, I walk across the hall, the first time I've gone over to the Sapientis' unit in months.

When Luca answers the door, his eyes zero in on Nathaniel standing behind me. "What do you want, Nate?"

"I don't want anything," Nathaniel replies smoothly, taking my hand in his. "This is all Joy's idea."

I glare at Luca, rooting myself to the floor with muscle spasms coursing through my legs. "Waiting a month to do this was generous."

That's when I punch him in the face.

He staggers backward, clutching his nose, his eyes shiny. He looks at me, speechless.

"How could you?" I spit out. "You knew how important

this was to me. But you only ever think about yourself," I finish, dropping my hand. I wave it; it stings from how hard I punched him. "Now, because of you, I need to come up with a *different* speech in the *fifteen minutes* it'll take us to get to the ceremony."

Beneath the late June sun in the middle of Central Park, Nathaniel and I are called to the stage to deliver our speeches.

I sit in the folding chair behind Nathaniel, looking out across a sea of purple robes, honors cords, mortarboards, and the families that have come to celebrate us. My moms and Nathaniel's family, the way it looks now—his siblings, his nieces and nephew, his sister-in-law, and his future brother-in-law—are right at the front.

"To the faculty and my fellow students of Caldwell Preparatory Academy," Nathaniel begins in his strong, confident voice. "Joy Corvi, you are an academic genius, and it was an honor to try to keep up with you these last four years." He looks over his shoulder at me, his eyes as bright as the blue sky above us.

I step up to the podium, waiting until I hear the squeak of Nathaniel sitting in the folding chair behind me to begin.

"Thank you, Nathaniel." I clear my throat, my left hand scrabbling at the podium as murmurs erupt throughout the crowd.

"I didn't know I was valedictorian until this morning," I

continue, "so, I don't have a big, wise speech prepared. But I know that valedictorian speeches are usually full of hopes and platitudes and reminiscing. In a way, because of our salutatorian, I will be doing exactly that. My hopes for the two of us are pretty close to my hopes for all the rest of you. I hope you've spent the last four years finding things: yourselves and your friends. I hope you all get to spend your time growing your passions. I hope you take the time to show your people how much you love them." I smile at Valentina and Yasmine, who smile back at me. "I hope you all find love and acceptance." I stop here to look at the people who have shown up here for me and Nathaniel. "Any and all kinds of it." Then I turn to look at Nathaniel, who has started to cry. "I hope you all feel valid and worthy enough to let that love in. Especially"—I tug at my rainbow cords—"if you are wearing these."

"And Nathaniel." My voice wavers as I start to cry myself. "I love you."

"Joy." Nathaniel gets to his feet to stand next to me, just as, in a way, he always has. "I love you so much." He says it loud enough that it carries through the microphone before pulling me in for a short kiss filled with so much.

When we break apart, I realize the whole crowd is cheering. So, I pull him closer—this boy I have spent the last four years of my life falling in love with—to kiss him again.

ONE YEAR LATER

NATHANIEL

The sun is just beginning to set in Central Park, turning the sky into an incredible painting of pale yellows, purples, and pinks.

Joy and I are traipsing across the lawn—me in a tuxedo with a purple tie, her in a matching dress and the pastel rainbow shawl her ma had knitted for her—toward the spot where Everett and Arthur are about to get married.

But Joy tugs on my elbow, and I stop walking.

"Are you all right?" I ask. "The grass isn't too hard to walk on, is it?"

"No." She shakes her head, barely hiding her smile. "It's not that. I—I have something to give you." From the inside pocket of her shawl—because her mothers are two of the most practical women I have ever met—she pulls out a piece of paper.

"Here." Her eyes gleam in the light of the sunset as she hands it to me. "Read it."

Dear Nathaniel,

I hope you don't mind me using your real name this time.

Today, we're headed to Central Park to watch Everett and Arthur get married, and I need to tell you that I love you.

You know this already, of course, as we say it every day. Multiple times a day.

At our first Pride parade together, wrapped up in a rainbow flag. During tearful airport goodbyes as we boarded our plane for California. While unpacking dorm rooms. After late-night study sessions. While splitting a cake on our nineteenth birthday and eating it on the floor of my dorm room.

We always ensure that we say those three simple words: "I love you."

So, as we're walking down that aisle, to watch your brother marry the man he loves, just know that I love you.

Will we have a day like this for ourselves someday?

Love,

Joy

"Joy." I tuck the paper into the inside pocket of my tuxedo. "You wrote me a love letter."

"I did." She withdraws a small packet of tissues from her

shawl next, wiping away the tears that have managed to trickle down my cheeks. "Because I love you. And I—I want our future to look like this."

"Yes," I say keeping my eyes on her. "Me too."

"So, we're on the same page," Joy murmurs. "Good. Now, let's go watch your brother get married."

JOY

Once Everett and Arthur are wed in a beautiful ceremony, they're almost immediately called to the dance floor.

"Hang on. Joy?" Arthur wheels over to where Nathaniel and I are standing at the edge of the dance floor. "Hold these?" He hands me his bouquet, a pretty collection of summer flowers.

"Of course," I say, smiling back at him. Arthur and I have bonded, particularly over the intersectionality of queerness and physical disability.

"Hey." Franny chuckles, balancing Natalie on her hip. "That bouquet is Joy's now."

"My fiancée is right," Daniel adds, kissing the top of her head.

"You're looking at her like she's hung the moon," Cillian says, grinning.

"That's the point of love," Declan says as Eitan squeezes his hand.

"You're as romantic as Nathaniel, you know that?" Vikram grins.

"I mean," Yasmine says, wrapping her arm around Val. "I'm pretty sure my girlfriend created this entire galaxy, so there's that."

"Supernovas included," Val adds happily, kissing her.

"Dance with me?" Nathaniel asks. I take his hand, and we walk over to an empty place on the floor. "You know . . ." Nathaniel wraps both of his arms around my soft waist, pulling me closer to him again. "Whoever catches the bouquet at a wedding reception is the next to get married."

"Why, Nathaniel," I murmur against his tuxedo. "Are you proposing right now?"

"No," he replies, gentle laughter in his voice. "We both know that our brains' frontal lobes aren't fully developed until we're twenty-five. So, I will plan to propose on our twenty-fifth birthday." He bends down to kiss me. "I love you, Joy."

I smile at him. "I love you too, Nathaniel."

ACKNOWLEDGMENTS

First, to my incredible agent and friend, Emily Forney. Emily, thank you for everything. This is the second book we've brought into the world together and I am so grateful to have you by my side. Your partnership, enthusiasm, excitement, and determination mean the world to me. We are truly the Darcey and Stacey Silva of publishing, and I cannot wait to see what we do next.

To my amazing editor, Tiffany Colón. Tiffany, working on *Love Letters for Joy* with you has been just as exciting as when we worked on *You, Me, and Our Heartstrings.* Thank you for getting to the heart of this love letter to queerness and disability with me.

I must also thank everyone at Scholastic, including Abigail McAden, David Levithan, Melissa Schirmer, Brooke Shearouse, Seale Ballenger, Victoria Velez, and the rest of the editorial, publicity, and marketing teams.

Thank you to Reen Mikhail and Cassy Price for another absolutely beautiful cover.

To my critique partner, Tia Bearden. Tia, my sunshine, my bestie friend, my one and only, my beloved. Thank you for that trip to our house in Tennessee in January of 2022, where we took the pitch for *Love Letters for Joy* and worked tirelessly on it for six straight days. From the whiteboards with the perfect titles—*The Times and Trials of Nathaniel Wright* being our favorite—to that fateful moment on the highway where you turned to me, smirked, and said, "Hear me out."

We changed this book's entire plot in the span of the five most adrenaline-fueled minutes of my life. But that change was exactly what this book needed.

I love you more than words can say.

To my critique partner, agent sibling, and best friend, Michelle Mohrweis. Michelle, you read nearly every single draft of this book, encouraging me with each chapter. Thank you for reassuring me and for helping me whenever I needed it. Love you!

Thank you to my author friends, Daniel Aleman, E.M. Anderson, Jen DeLuca, Marissa Eller, Jonny Garza Villa, Eric Geron, Mary Lynne Gibbs, Jason June, Brian D. Kennedy, Libby Kennedy, Hanna Kim, Lillie Lainoff, Cara Liebowitz, Brittany Machado, Lucy Mason, Briana Miano, Riss M. Neilson, Gabe Netz, Sabina Nordqvist, Skye Quinlan, Christen Randall, and Rachel Lynn Solomon.

Thank you to Jessica Lemmons for always indulging my love of theatre.

To my Authors Play D&D crew: Again, Cara, Christen, Jonny, and Michelle, as well as our incomparable Dungeon Master, Jarred. Thank you for the raspberry squares, apple ciders, borscht, and the thriving yak business. I couldn't be more grateful for our adventures—and the anchor that Dungeons & Dragons is in my life because of you. I love you!

Thank you to Leanne and Callum Simpson for letting me draft a portion of this book on your couch—and making sure we played board games.

Thank you to my best friends Eric Rittle, Leah Rittle, and Dr. Mert Keçeli for a friendship that I am endlessly grateful for, whether we're unpacking my apartment until 9:00 p.m. or seeing a movie. (An extra thank-you to Mert for answering all my medical questions for this book.)

Thank you to Shala Haslam, the best buddy-reading companion I could ever ask for.

Thank you to the Cute Crew—Brenna, Dylan, Gwen, Morgan, Shannah, and Val—for everything. I still think about that 10:30 p.m. IHOP trip.

Thank you to my family for loving me, encouraging me, and knowing that being an author was what I was always meant to do. I love you all so much. I must also thank my cat, Miles, as he always seems to know when I need him to curl up in my lap.

And lastly, to all the disabled, queer readers who found themselves in *Love Letters for Joy*: I hope you know that you are worthy of love.

Read on for a sneak peek at Melissa See's first book

YOU, ME, AND OUR HEARTSTRINGS

CHAPTER ONE

DAISY

I stumble into the orchestra room after fifth-chair violinist—and ever-present thorn in my side—Beaux Beckworth sticks his leg out across the doorway.

"Sorry, Differently Abled." He tries to sing the nickname he's had for me our entire four years at this academy, but Beaux is the sort of person who doesn't even tune his strings properly. So, he can't exactly carry a tune, either.

"Ha." I smooth down the skirt of my long-sleeved paisley-patterned dress as cerebral palsy makes a muscle spasm crawl up my left leg. "You're so funny, using my initials like that."

I hurry across the linoleum floor to the storage room, where all the violins, violas, basses, and cellos are kept.

Beaux mumbles something about me being second chair, but before I even push through the door, I hear another voice: It's low, like the G string on my own violin that's waiting for me inside.

“Are you okay?” Turning on my heel, I meet Noah Moray’s eyes and do a double take. Beneath a head of dark brown hair, they’re as blue as the forget-me-nots Ma had in stock at her flower shop last month, even behind tortoiseshell glasses.

Noah is the first-chair cellist, and probably the most talented person at this academy. He also rarely talks to anyone.

I’ve heard him play hundreds of times. But that doesn’t mean I’m immune to how brilliant a musician he is.

Or that I’ll admit how much I like hearing his voice. Same as the music he plays, it makes my stomach flutter each time I get to listen. Not that I’d ever *tell* Noah this, of course.

“Yeah.” I swallow past a slight lump in my throat. My heart thrums in my chest, and my cheeks warm with a blush. “I’m all right.”

I quickly duck into the storage room, grab my violin case from its cubby, and rush back to my seat.

“Hello, everyone!” our conductor trills, actually hitting the notes, unlike Beaux. Ms. Silverstein is one of the youngest teachers at the academy, but also one of the most skilled. She played Éponine on Broadway for a season and performed with the Opera Orchestra of New York.

We chorus our hellos back to her, and she perches on the edge of her desk. “First, I want to congratulate you all on a spectacular run of *Fiddler on the Roof.* You were all amazing. Now . . .” She claps her hands, beaming. “It’s time to talk about the winter holiday concert!”

Murmurs erupt around the room. The Manhattan Academy of Musical Performance's winter holiday concert is the biggest event of the year, where the band, musical theater, and orchestra students get to take the stage for the night. It's a chance to showcase our skill to the public, music conservatory professionals, and principal conductors. It could be my one shot at getting into Juilliard.

I shift in my seat. Juilliard's my dream. I sent in my prescreening audition back in September. I'm not fooling myself; even on the off chance I did get accepted, my family would never be able to afford the tuition. But this is my chance for a Juilliard faculty member to see me as a skilled disabled violinist—instead of the charity case who got accepted to this school on a scholarship because of my disability.

Maybe that would be enough to earn me a live audition.

I glance across the room at Noah, who's watching Ms. Silverstein with rapt attention, clutching the neck of his cello. Noah's from one of the most illustrious music families in all of New York City. Combined with him being a prodigy? He could probably just walk right into my top-choice college.

That thought makes a kaleidoscope of butterflies flutter in my stomach.

Besides, Noah just looks so handsome, so intense when he plays, creating beautiful music with every press of his strings, every stroke of his bow . . .

"The concert is going to be on December eleventh this year."

Ms. Silverstein's voice brings me back to the orchestra room. "We're, of course, performing a song as an orchestra. But before we dive into options, there is another component." She hops off her desk, walks around to the back of it, pulls open a drawer, and takes out a clipboard. A hush settles over us. "As you know, every year musicians from the orchestra, band, and musical theater are selected to perform duets. There are only four duets, so being chosen is huge.

"I have the duet assignments right here." Our conductor's smile sends another wave of whispers across the room. My best friend, Mazhar Tilki, leans over to say something to me, but I don't quite catch it. My left hand contracts around my bow frog instead.

"Are you ready?" Ms. Silverstein tucks a strand of dark brown curls behind her ear. We say yes, and she clears her throat. "In order of performance: Mazhar Tilki and Eric Zhao."

"Mazhar!" We wrap each other up into a quick hug amid the applause. But it's no surprise he got picked. He's the first-chair violinist and the best one at this academy. From across the room, cellist Eric cups their hands around their mouth and yells to Mazhar: "Ready for this?"

"Absolutely!" Mazhar replies.

Ms. Silverstein moves on down her list, but I tune her out—it's not like I'll be picked anyway. My best friend getting a spot is enough for me.

"And lastly!" she says. "Daisy Abano and Noah Moray."